SOHO TEEN

Dear Reader,

If you're already familiar with Margaux Froley's stellar debut, *Escape Theory*, then you're already aware of 17-year-old Devon Mackintosh—outsider, reluctant sleuth, and peer counselor at the prestigious Keaton School—as well as the praise *Escape Theory* has garnered: a starred review in *Publishers Weekly*, gushing blurbs from Cecily von Ziegesar and Sara Shepard, et cetera.

So without offering any spoilers, I'll keep this introduction short. *Hero Complex* is not only a novel that can be read and enjoyed on its own—rare for a sequel—but one that deftly explores a variety of historical and controversial issues that even as Margaux's huge fan and editor, I didn't see coming. After the first read, I had to reread right away, already knowing the twists and turns because I wanted to feel as smart as Margaux. Mystery and thriller lovers, you know what I'm talking about. It's pretty much the highest praise I can offer an author.

I hope you find Devon's newest journey as compelling as I did.

Sincerely,
Daniel Ehrenhaft
Editorial Director, Soho Teen
Soho Press / 853 Broadway, New York, NY 10003
212.260.1900 / dehrenhaft@sohopress.com
www.sohoteen.com

Also by Margaux Froley

Escape Theory

HERO COMPLEX

margaux froley

SOHO
TEEN

Copyright © 2014 by Soho Press, Inc. and Margaux Froley

All rights reserved.

Published in the United States in 2014 by Soho Teen
an imprint of
Soho Press, Inc.
853 Broadway
New York, NY 10003

Library of Congress Cataloging-in-Publication Data

TK

ISBN 978-1-61695-320-1
eISBN 978-1-61695-321-8

Interior design by Janine Agro, Soho Press, Inc.

Printed in the United States of America

10 9 8 7 6 5 4 3 2 1

Dedi tk

HERO COMPLEX: A psychological syndrome with the noble impulse
to come to the rescue of sufferers even when there is no necessity.*

* *The Archetypes and the Collective Unconscious: The Collected Works of C.G. Jung* by Carl Gustav Jung

PROLOGUE

December 31, 2012
San Francisco Bay

The limo had seemed excessive. That was even before Devon boarded the 250-foot mega yacht—where she handed her overnight bag to her personal butler, slipped on a hand-beaded Marchesa gown, and requested a song from the children's choir singing the Rolling Stones catalogue: "Moonlight Mile." It seemed an appropriate song for the moonlit waters of the San Francisco Bay on New Year's Eve.

Cleo called the yacht party "Dad's New Year's Circus Spectacular." For Devon it might as well have been a trip to the moon itself. A welcome one. After everything that had happened on the Keaton hillside, Devon needed an escape. With twelve bedrooms for guests and enough bunks for twenty crewmembers, the yacht was a study in Cleo Lambert's world, full of secret compartments and hidden rooms. Already Devon had accidentally turned on a television (the screen took up the entire wall of her bedroom) and found a room full of scuba gear just by trying to flip on a light in the bathroom. Everything onboard, from the cup holders to the infinity swimming pool, had the ability to be tucked away, strapped down, or folded up. If only experiences could be compartmentalized as neatly.

Outside on the second-level deck, Devon could watch the choir singing on the smaller deck above. Their conductor, scruffy looking but with infinite patience for his twenty young singers—probably an elementary school teacher in his regular life—had donned a black tux, but Devon noticed he wore frayed black Converse. A nice reminder that most people weren't dining on $500 white truffle risotto balls at home. But tonight wasn't about the constant class war Devon fought to ignore at Keaton. Tonight, she was happy to forget. Yes, these people tipped their gardeners more than her mom probably made all year. But tonight she was one of them, part of the 1 percent. She would gladly play her Cinderella role at the ball knowing pumpkin time was inevitable.

There was a sharp elbow at her side.

"They are pouring Dom like it's Jay-Z's birthday," Cleo said, juggling three
bubbling flutes.

"Took you long enough," Devon ribbed, relieving Cleo of one of the glasses.

"Hey, manage the 'tude. I had to squeeze this dress past all of these bloated idiots, flirt with the bartender, avoid my dad, *and* make it back up to this deck without spillage. Now, a toast to an awesome 2013 full of bigger, better, and brighter. *À la vôtre.*" She clinked glasses with Devon. "And to maybe a little less drama this year, too, *n'est-ce pas.*" Cleo clinked glasses again.

"Cheers." Devon smiled in agreement. "Less drama would be nice."

Both of them glanced at the puncture mark still healing on

Devon's wrist. The thin sleeves on her dress couldn't fully hide the red scar that might never fade.

"But this is exactly what the doctor ordered, right?" Cleo said, as if speaking louder would keep their heads from going *there*, the night Devon was working hard to forget. *There*, the realization that they had drawn out a murderer. *There*, the memory that Eric Hutchins has killed his own younger brother, Hutch. *There*, Devon finally accepting the loss of her first love, the guy that all future guys would be compared against. *There*.

Knowing Eric was behind Hutch's death didn't bring Devon the satisfaction she had hoped for. Whatever answers Hutch was looking for, they were beyond Devon's reach. All she could do now was let go. Let it all go.

Cleo flicked a nail against Devon's glass. "Got somewhere else to be?"

Devon fought to stay present, but the storm cloud of thoughts kept swirling, building pressure in her head, as they always did. Eric Hutchins had murdered his only brother, universally loved, to protect his share of the land on the Keaton hill. And their grandfather, Reed Hutchins, had warned Devon of an impending battle between the Hutchins and Dover families. But why? Eric Hutchins and Maya Dover had been hiding their relationship—naturally because of Maya's pregnancy.

When Devon confronted Maya with what she knew about Eric, their age—

Maya still under eighteen) seemed to be the least of Maya's worries. The battle between their two families loomed largest. Devon still didn't understand how that was possible. If *she* were pregnant in high school, the last thing she'd care about was her family history. Then again, she didn't come from a family with history like Maya's. (Or like Cleo's, for that matter.) Devon still felt like she had blinders over her eyes so she could only see the small bits of information in front of her. There was so much more on the periphery.

Every time she turned her head to get a better look, the most vital parts remained just out of her vision. Whatever it was, whatever this elusive thing that had divided two families, pitted brother against brother, whatever it was . . . Hutch had died for it.

"This is great. Really," Devon forced herself to respond. "Although I'm going to start thinking that all champagne is supposed to taste like this." She took a big sip, resisting the dry tickle of bubbles behind her nose.

"Doesn't it?" Cleo laughed. "Okay, so what's the game plan? The bartender on the lower deck is totally cute, and we had a little eye-contact moment. But did you see that cater waiter in the entertainment room?"

Devon could only laugh, too. *Entertainment room. This whole yacht is one big entertainment room.* "Was that the room with the spiral staircase?"

"No, try to keep up. The entertainment room had the pinball machine and eight-foot flat screen."

"Right, how could I forget?"

"No, seriously, the waiter walking around with the tuna tartare. Blond. Dimples. I'm a total sucker for a guy with dimples. And tartare."

"Say 'tartare' one more time," Devon said.

"Tartare." Cleo shrugged. "Why?"

"I just wanted you to hear yourself." Devon broke into a fit of giggles.

"You're avoiding the subject. We've got to find someone to kiss at midnight, or else our year will be boy-less. It's a New Year's rule or curse. I don't know. One of them."

"I thought you already had a boy." More than ever, Devon envied Cleo's lightness, her ability to float between people and places without getting stuck or bogged down in anyone else's sticky issues.

"Bodhi?" Cleo took a long swig of her champagne. "Yeah, he's been fun, but he's not here, is he? And we need to appease the gods of New Year's Eve. Must kiss a boy at midnight or be forever cursed. Drink up."

Devon couldn't help but look around just in case. "Are you sure your dad is cool with this?"

"Ha! You think my dad has time to stop and care about us having a glass or two—"

"Or three."

"Or three on New Year's Eve. He's making all his deals for next year tonight." Cleo downed her champagne and split the remaining third glass into their flutes.

Devon exhaled at the refill. "I'm getting a little light-headed." She tried to hand her glass to Cleo.

"That's the point," Cleo said, pushing the glass back. "What good is peer pressure if it doesn't work? Finish up. Then let's find you a waiter to kiss at midnight. I got dibs on Dimples." Cleo gave Devon a quick wink, grabbed a handful of her black billowing gown, and led Devon below deck.

THE PARTY WAS DEAFENING downstairs. A deejay danced in front of his computer, and hidden speakers pumped jazzy techno (*was that even a real genre?*) into the dense room. Devon took in the herd of gray-haired men in black tuxes, clinking ice cubes and golden liquor. The women were all clones, too: sculpted hairstyles and jewel-colored dresses, always laughing at the right times, an eye on their men for the correct social cues.

Cleo pulled Devon toward a mirrored hallway behind the staircase. "I think the waiters are using the deck off the navigation room as a smoking lounge," she said. "And if they're taking a break, they've got time to chat with us."

Devon let go of Cleo and caught a glimpse of herself in the chorus line of reflections down the hall. Uh-oh. She now realized what the wind had been doing to her hair. *That's what I get for trying to copy an updo from YouTube.*

"Be right there," she called.

She attempted to tuck the flyaways back into the knot on the top of her head. The party chatter outside was getting louder, and Devon could hear splashes of water. But the splashes sounded like they were coming from inside the boat. How was that possible?

Devon gave up on her hair and continued along the hallway toward a double door.

Where had Cleo disappeared? The mirrors echoed Devon's reflection into infinity. Maybe she had to walk through these doors?

Devon tiptoed into a bedroom suite that seemed to be designed exclusively for architectural magazines, rock stars, and movie drug lords. A creamy white bedspread and perfectly pressed pillows. White lacquer walls lined with drawers and cubbies. A white leather bench beside a stocked wet bar. The ceiling made entirely of glass . . .

With a laugh, Devon realized she was looking up at the bottom of the swimming pool on the deck above. Bare legs kicked and rippled through the water. Waves of purple-and-red light danced across the bedspread, blasted from the outdoor lighting. A silver plastic *Happy New Year!* kazoo drifted to the bottom of the pool and rested next to a broken tiara simply stating *Happy New Y*.

Another splash, and another girl went into the water. Her red dress fanned out around her like a life-size lily pad. A silver sequined heel clunked down against the bottom of the pool in slow motion, landing with a muffled thud. Devon reached up and could almost touch the glass above. It was like being inside a snow globe, except this snow globe was filled with leather banquettes and a revolving liquor cabinet.

"Pretty insane, right?"

A waiter in a white jacket stood at the entrance to the room, an empty tray hanging by his side. Devon dropped her hands, feeling like she'd been caught doing something wrong. But no, she was the guest here.

"Yeah, I guess. I mean, once you've seen one glass-bottomed pool on a yacht, you've seen them all, right?"

The waiter laughed a little, revealing a perfect dimple on each cheek. Cleo's waiter. But where was Cleo?

"You don't know where the navigation room is, do you? I got a little lost down here. I'm Devon, by the way." She hurried across the room to shake his hand. Best to be formal.

"Eli," he said with a puzzled smile, giving her hand a quick shake. "You mean, this room?" He pressed a panel in the white lacquer wall next to Devon, and it popped open. "I gotta get back to the bar, but happy New Year, Devon."

Eli gave Devon one last glance at those dimples before disappearing back into the hallway. *Typical Cleo*, she thought. *Of course there was a secret door and she didn't tell me. Probably watching from some hidden camera while I figure it out.*

Devon stepped past the panel. Screens glowed in the small dark room: black-and-white footage of various parts of the yacht. Another screen, all in blue, displayed graphs charting the yacht's trip, knots traveled or something else water related. Devon didn't speak "yacht."

On a shelf at eye level was an antique spyglass. Copper with hints of green, fighting the oxidation from the salty sea air. In her imagination, yachting still involved things like spyglasses and rum and wooden legs. Okay, maybe she was just thinking of pirates now.

She looked again at the screens, where a blinking dot slowly moved in the bay. She shook her head; staring at the screens was making her vision blurry. Or was it the champagne? She felt a chill from the outside air. There across the room was another door, and beyond it probably Cleo sitting on a balcony, flirtatiously taking a drag off a waiter's cigarette. Devon steadied herself against the wall of monitors. She wished Cleo had warned her that wearing heels while yachting was a bad idea. *Is yachting even a real verb?*

"Were you trying to lose me?" she asked as she opened the balcony door.

But she was talking to empty sea air. No Cleo. No smokers' lounge for the waiters. The party continued to roar on the other side of the boat, and the wind whipped past her ears, loud and cold. Before she could turn around, Devon felt a hard crack against the back of her skull. The pain deep, yet distant. As a tremor shot through her body, the moon went fuzzy, and everything sounded thick, an underwater dream in Devon's personal snow globe. A flicker in her vision, and the green metal spyglass flew overboard and landed in the water. The splash was absorbed by the moving boat. Shoes squeaked on the deck behind her. White, rubber. White sleeves opening a door. Someone had hit her and left. And now the metal railing was coming toward her. Fast.

Put a hand out. Catch yourself! she commanded her body. But her hands didn't respond. And when her cheek connected with the railing, the pain was immediate. A flash of red light, the image of the *Happy New Y* tiara. *Happy New Y, indeed.* Just before everything went dark, Devon could have sworn she heard a snippet of that song she loved: "*I'm just about a moonlight mile on down . . .*"

CHAPTER 1

"But I still don't understand why Mr. Robins isn't here." Devon ran her hand across the blue suede couch cushion. Stacks of books on the floor leaned against the wall in mini towers. One push and they would all fall like dominoes. Her cheek burned at the thought of falling. The bump under her right eye had subsided, but the bruise was still a deep purple. And the large lump under her hair on the back of her head still ached if she pressed it hard enough.

Across the small office, Dr. Jocelyn Hsu tucked her legs under her in the large leather chair. She pulled a knitted throw blanket across her lap and took a sip of her tea. "Well, I can explain it again if you want. But there isn't much more information I can give you. Headmaster Wyler and a few other concerned advisors, including Mr. Robins himself, thought he could use some additional support around here."

Devon nodded. "Go on."

"Well, given that you and Mr. Robins were working somewhat closely together last semester, it seemed appropriate that you now work with someone who might bring a fresh perspective to things. So that's where I come in." Dr. Hsu smiled warmly.

For someone who seemed to enjoy cozy blankets, thick wool socks, and flowing blouses, Dr. Hsu's hairdo was a surprisingly sharp and stylish bob cut. She probably had it done in San Francisco as opposed to the hippie salons in Santa Cruz, Devon thought. That was definitely not a ten-dollar Monte Vista barbershop visit.

"Do you think you'll be okay with that?" Dr. Hsu smiled again, but Devon could see her pressing her lips together, waiting for an answer.

Devon had been noticing that smile a lot lately. From her mom, holding her hand at the hospital while asking her to explain the yacht attack yet again. From Presley, urging Devon to tell her anything she wanted. Everyone wanted Devon to talk about the assault over and over again. From the police and doctors, too—everyone had a different version of the "understanding smile." In the short week since her attack, Devon had told the story more times than she could remember.

Thankfully Cleo had stepped in and soaked up most the attention in her role as Devon's Knight in Shining Armor. She'd found Devon unconscious on the deck that night, the one place on the yacht without security cameras. Naturally there would be no proof of Devon's claim that someone had clubbed her from behind. There seemed to be a quiet understanding between Cleo's father and Devon's mom that Devon had sneaked a few glasses of champagne, gotten tipsy, and fallen down. Devon's insistence that she didn't "eat rail," as Presley termed it, just brought on more tight smiles. The police had real cases to solve, and Cleo's father didn't want any bad publicity about an underage girl getting drunk at his company's yacht party.

But Cleo alone had never given Devon an understanding smile. She knew there was nothing to be patient about, nothing to politely endure while the story unfolded. No, what had happened was somehow personal and deliberate. Cleo knew, too, that this wasn't an accident. Devon also suspected—though Cleo never admitted as much—that Cleo might have even felt responsible. She'd let Devon out of her sight. She'd traipsed ahead, happy and drunk, oblivious to lurking danger.

Besides, the attack had shaken the politeness out of Devon. Life was too short to follow rules anymore. She needed to get answers and wasn't worried about stepping on anyone's toes along the way.

"You don't have to pretend that I have a choice in this," she said to Dr. Hsu.

The woman's smile didn't falter, but she tilted her head to the side. "Oh, of course you have a choice whether you want to see me or not. Except you're smart. You also know that your choice comes with conditions. Keaton can't reinstate the peer counseling program until I've given my vote of approval."

"What else is new? I play ball with you guys, or I can kiss my Stanford rec letter goodbye."

Dr. Hsu shrugged but kept smiling. Professional yet understanding, Devon thought. The recipe for a good counselor. "Who says I even want to be a peer counselor again?" Devon asked.

"I don't know. No one. You, maybe. It's your choice."

"Choices again. Nice." Devon let out a short laugh.

Dr. Hsu sipped her tea. Waiting. Devon knew the waiting game. Let the subject talk about what they want; it's more revealing. Dr. Hsu's haircut was too expensive for someone who didn't take this job seriously. Hell, she'd earned a Ph.D. in psychotherapy; she probably wouldn't cave until Devon said something first.

"You want me to talk about the attack, huh?"

"If you want." Another sip of tea.

"I didn't see him. I didn't notice anything weird earlier in the night. I've been through all of that. Someone hit me. There's nothing else to tell."

"There's still you, your experience of the night. Plus, we know that you were drinking at the time, so maybe your experience is, let's say, *heightened*."

Devon blinked rapidly. "Heightened? You ever been attacked? It happens so fast, but time slows down. It's hard to explain. One minute I can't find Cleo, another I'm on some secret deck, and someone hits me hard. I could have gone overboard. It would have been so easy. 'Girl gets drunk, falls over side of boat at night.' No noise, no light. I wouldn't be here. I'm sure that was their plan. Someone didn't want me to be here."

"And by someone, you mean your *attacker*?"

Devon shook her head and laughed. "I see what you did there. You say *attacker* like it's in quotes. Like that part is still up for debate. My *alleged attacker*."

Dr. Hsu leaned forward, gripping her mug with both hands. "Well, let's discuss the facts. Cleo found you; there was a 911 call. The yacht immediately came back to shore. What happened then?"

"Look, I know it sounds far-fetched." Devon maintained eye contact with Dr. Hsu. It was important that she not present like she was lying or uncomfortable with the truth.

"Devon, the police met the boat at the dock. Everyone was cleared. So either the attacker was a guest at the party, or what? He jumped overboard in the middle of the night in the bay? Yes, I'll be the one to say it. What you're proposing does sound far-fetched. That's why people are worried about you. Do you want to talk about how much you had to drink that night? Have you been drinking beyond just that night?"

"That's not the issue here." Devon fought to keep her voice even. "What happened wasn't random. I know there's more to this; I just don't know what yet. The last time I felt like this . . ." She didn't finish the thought. It would make her sound paranoid.

"Yes, tell me about last time." Dr. Hsu leaned back, adjusted the blanket over her lap, and took another sip of tea.

Devon paused. Dr. Hsu had clearly been warned about Devon. But how? Was the school pitching Devon as some sort of paranoid rogue they needed to tame? She had been right about Hutch despite everything Robins had said about her theories. Yet somehow she was being painted as the delusional one here still.

"You think I'm imagining things? Like, someone is out to get me?"

"No, not at all," Dr. Hsu quickly replied. "If someone was out to get you, this is a very real post-traumatic stress reaction. I'm just trying to understand why you feel that one person is part of something larger."

Devon lowered her eyes. "Last time, when Hutch died, no one believed me. This feels the same, like there's more than just this one incident. I don't know how I know, I just do. There's more to it."

Dr. Hsu nodded. "But this isn't last time."

"I didn't say it was. It's *like* last time." Devon pushed her shoulders back and sat up straighter. Dr. Hsu was not going to twist her words around.

"Okay. Tell me more about Hutch. About your relationship with him."

"I'm sure Headmaster Wyler told you everything you need to know about Hutch and what happened. It's been in all the papers."

"Yes, but I want to hear it from you."

Devon bit her thumbnail. It was pointless to attempt to convince Dr. Hsu of anything. Apparently the brass at Keaton had a specific idea of what Devon's issues were.

Fine, if she couldn't change their minds, she might as well use their preconceived notions to her advantage. While their version of Paranoid Devon spun in circles, Real Devon could focus on finding her attacker. Raven and Bodhi were already hacking into the records of the yacht catering company. But that wasn't appropriate

conversation for therapy, was it? No, she could be the Devon that
Keaton wanted her to be right now.

For the first time, she smiled at Dr. Hsu.

Game on.

CHAPTER 2

Devon was one of the early arrivals in the dining hall on Saturday morning. She had been awake since 7 A.M. Sleeping until noon would have been a luxurious waste of the day, but her body would not comply. So she'd rolled out of bed, pulled on her Keaton hoodie, retied the drawstring on her plaid flannel pajama pants, and slipped into her battered Uggs. It was Saturday morning; bras were optional as far as she was concerned.

The good news about Keaton was that weekend mornings were generally an all-out call for sloppiness. It's not like they wore starched uniforms during the school week, but after five eighteen-hour days in a row, Saturdays warranted pajamas.

While the kitchen staff poured steaming potatoes and silver-dollar pancakes into the waiting vats at the food counter, Devon opted for the cereal island. Froot Loops, Lucky Charms, Cocoa Puffs,

Cheerios, granola, and Corn Flakes. All freshmen tended to fill up on the Froot Loops and Lucky Charms. Maybe it was that early taste of freedom from parents choosing healthier cereal—or just a sugar radar that was more finely tuned the younger you were— but everyone consistently started with the full-sugar cereals. When the rebellious fun dimmed, their breakfast choices became plainer. Devon had indulged in her Lucky Charms phase and was happy to put it, and the memory of all that purple milk, behind her. Now like most juniors, she was a Corn Flakes girl.

Seated at an empty table in the back, she dug into her bowl of cereal. From this vantage point she had a clear view of Presley— also in pajamas and Uggs—strolling through the doors and filling up a plate with pancakes. *Weird*, Devon thought with a smile. She expected Presley to be in a soccer uniform or running gear. Winter was her prime time to show off her athletic skills, and she usually spent her free time training.

Devon wasn't getting a soccer scholarship anywhere; that much was certain. No, instead of pretending that she had any inclination to be a future all-star, Devon was happy with "self-directed gym" or "Approved Slacker Hour," as she looked at it. It had to be the easiest sports assignment in school. Only juniors and seniors were allowed to sign up. Go to the school gym for an hour and sign an attendance sheet. That was it. No teacher supervision, no uniforms. While most of the school ran laps, drills, and scored goals, Devon could pretend to do yoga or simply read a book in the corner near a weight machine. Presley, on the other hand, was actually ranked in California as a top soccer player. Colleges would be vying to give her a scholarship.

"Last Saturday before the gauntlet of crazy," Presley explained, answering Devon's unspoken question as she plunked her tray down on the table. "I'm about to lose all my weekends for the next four months. Can we please have a girls' date today?"

Devon smirked. She let her remaining Corn Flakes go soggy before answering. "Depends. What does this girls' date entail?"

"Well, first off, we get back to where we were," Presley said. "Things haven't been the same since last semester, and I kinda still hate myself for . . . you know, doubting. Hutch. Can we please get our nails done and get a picnic from the deli and eat too many carbs while ogling surfers down at the Cove?"

Perfect. It was their favorite Saturday ritual, dating back from their freshman year. Granted, those deli sandwiches were partly to blame for both Devon and Presley gaining a few of their freshman fifteen, but those early weekends on the beach marked the beginning of their friendship. Who else could Devon talk to with equal intensity about the value of a good sharp cheddar cheese and the hilarity of surfers who tried to peel themselves out of soaked wetsuits and look cool at the same time?

"If those carbs are attached to a deli sandwich, then, yeah, I'm in."

Presley clapped her hands together. "Cool! I gotta go for a run, do some laundry, but meet you for the twelve-P.M. bus into town. We're gonna have some fuuuh-uuuun!" She swung her head from side to side, singing the last word.

Devon felt something hopeful stir inside. Pretty much everything with Presley was *fuuh-uuuun!*, even the way she used her hands to dip each pancake into a puddle of syrup before stuffing it into her mouth. But Devon hadn't heard the word in a while. Hutch's death had drawn a before-and-after line in their friendship. Before, Devon figured that she and Presley would be inseparable. College, first jobs, boyfriends, future husbands, weddings, kids . . . there was Presley alongside her. After, Devon had to face the reality that maybe this friend wouldn't have her back unconditionally. Was this an attempt to reclaim their "before" friendship?

But that wasn't the question that mattered, and Devon knew it. There was only one question: Was that even possible?

BAY HOUSE WAS JUST stirring to life as Devon left her room to meet Presley at the bus pickup. The sound of a lone shower running, the chatter of girls talking in the laundry room, and a movie playing on someone's computer trickled into the hallway. But when male voices joined the chorus, Devon slowed her pace. Where was that coming from? Boys weren't allowed inside a girls' dorm at this time of day. She heard the bang of drawers opening and closing. Near the end of the hall, a door was wide open.

Maya's.

Devon peeked inside. Two movers, burly guys in matching yellow T-shirts, were taping boxes closed. The mattress was bare, the walls blank. Even the desk looked cleaned off. Maya wouldn't be coming back to Keaton, Devon realized. She knew Maya might be taking time off because of her pregnancy, but Devon thought there was always hope of her returning. In one quiet Saturday morning Maya's existence would be wiped out of Keaton history.

Outside Devon saw the U-Move-It van in the dorm driveway. A black Mercedes was parked next to it, a woman in the driver's seat talking on her cell phone. Her black hair fell perfectly around her shoulders, and her deep brown eyes looked just like Maya's. Devon recognized her instantly from the Internet and magazine articles: it was C.C. Tran, Maya's mom and wife to pharmaceutical titan Edward Dover. They locked eyes.

Devon gave her a tight smile, which C.C. returned just as tightly. Devon couldn't imagine what that woman must be going through: her teenage daughter pregnant, dropping out of school, and having a baby with an accused murderer, the scion of a family rival, no less. *I thought my family dinners sucked.* It seemed impolite to stare, so Devon continued her way up the hill to meet Presley.

As the Keaton bus shifted gears on its drive down the hillside into Monte Vista, Presley turned in her seat to face Devon. "I had an idea over break. It's kind of amazing, but you're going to have to get your mom on board."

"On board for what?" Devon asked. She saw where this was going—permission slips of some sort.

"What if we went on our college trip together? Maybe you and your mom and me and my mom? We could do a few schools around New York and Vermont. A little East Coast tour. Wouldn't that be the best trip ever?" Presley's blonde curls bounced with each word.

Every junior at Keaton was planning a productive spring break. Either they were touring college campuses, or they were doing something to boost their applications, like working in a Honduran orphanage or organizing a glitzy fundraiser to promote early cancer screenings. Just last night, Devon overheard Sima Park down the hall asking her roommate which shoes were more appropriate for hanging out with orphans, Toms or Birkenstocks. (Sima voted Toms, ultimately. Double do-gooding, she reasoned.)

Devon, meanwhile, had far overshot her goal of using the Keaton peer counselor program as an extracurricular bonus. Of course, the irony was too twisted for her to consider for very long without feeling sick. But there was no denying it; Hutch's death would help her in terms of getting into a good college.

Beyond just bragging rights for being Keaton's first peer counselor, she'd picked up some local notoriety for her involvement with sniffing out his murderer. The *Santa Cruz Sentinel* had run a small column about Devon as Keaton's first peer counselor turned live-action sleuth. Devon's problem wasn't so much what to write about herself but how to approach the delicate subject of boosting her self-image through others' pain. She'd long stopped Googling herself—which probably wasn't a good thing. But what else could she do, when Hutch's name always appeared with hers?

"Besides," Presley continued in Devon's protracted silence, "we totally have to scope out which school has the hottest guys. 'Cause you know I'm a sucker for a guy in a peacoat. And the one thing we can count on during spring on the East Coast? Peacoats. It'll be like living in the fall/winter J.Crew catalog. Yummy."

"You already live there," Devon cracked. It was true; Presley's dorm room walls were adorned with J.Crew catalog pages of men wearing black and blue peacoats—handsome, yet slightly chilly. This was her new type.

"So what do you say?"

"Yeah, that could be fun. I'll talk to my mom," Devon said.

Presley clapped again. Devon smiled but couldn't muster up the same excitement. She had been so focused on Stanford, it hadn't occurred to her to look elsewhere. But maybe Presley was right. Maybe Devon should keep her options open. Although a guy in a peacoat was out of the question.

THE SANDWICHES WERE PERFECT. Devon hadn't had her favorite once this entire year, the roast beef with cheddar on pumpernickel bread, which was tantamount to a crime. She and Presley had their sandwiches wrapped to go. (Presley stuck with her favorite, the turkey and cranberry "for old times' sake.") They walked the few blocks to the beach and found a comfortable set of boulders to lean against while they ate and watched the surfers.

"If you watch them long enough, you feel like you're bobbing along the top of the ocean like they are," Devon said between bites.

"What's up with you going all surfer-centric on me?" Presley asked. "First you're friends with the Elliots, next you'll be joining the morning surf van."

Devon finished chewing. "And you're saying that's a bad thing?"

"Hey, I didn't say it was good or bad. You're just different. I feel like I used to be able to read your mind, but now you seem kind of lost at sea, like you're just drifting through everything. Or maybe it's just me." Presley slapped Devon's leg. "Come on, admit it. You over me? You found someone else?"

Now Devon had to laugh. Only Presley could cut to the heart of what was happening between them. "Pres, you know you're my first love. There's nobody else but you. Well, you and some tasty waves," she added in a stoner surfer voice. "Hope that's copacetic, dude." She wadded up her sandwich wrapper and tossed it at Presley's head.

"You two being Surf Betties today?"

Devon squinted up to see Raven Elliot standing in front of them in the sand. Raven's signature dreadlocks were wrapped into a beehive shape at the top of her head. Her wetsuit hung at her waist, a black swim shirt with a Rip Curl logo across her chest, and her wax-riddled surfboard under one arm.

Devon really hoped Raven hadn't overheard her "tasty waves" joke. "Hey, Raven! Yeah, we're just here to make sure everyone's behaving out there on the water."

"Yeah, 'cause if they're not, they're gonna have to answer to me." Presley held up a menacing fist.

Raven giggled. "You see Bodhi out there?"

"Wasn't looking. But don't think he's out there," Devon replied.

Raven looked at Presley and bit her lip. "You know, he wanted to talk to you. About the yacht crew from New Year's. We found something. Well, Bodhi found it mostly. I just pulled some video files."

Devon heard an overloud sigh next to her. Suddenly Presley was standing up. "Okay, Veronica Mars. I'll leave you to your investigations—"

"Wait," Devon pleaded. Presley turned, and Devon saw the look in her eyes. She didn't want to be a part of this. There was no point in asking Presley to stay; this was the line their friendship didn't cross. "I'm sorry, but I have to deal with this . . ."

Presley nodded. "I get it. You got to scratch that itch."

"Pres," Devon began, "this is real. Something happened, and I have to find out who's behind it."

"I know you do. It's just . . . I miss the old you. I want that girl back, ya know?"

Devon swallowed. "I miss her, too, Presley. I'd love the old me back, but that ship has sailed. Besides, it's not like I chose this."

"Didn't you?" Presley asked as she slung her backpack over her shoulder. "I'll see you back on campus." She carried her shoes as she walked down the beach to the parking lot.

Devon watched her go, stunned. How could her best friend not even care what had happened? But worse, maybe she'd just lost interest in Devon.

"Let her go," Raven said. "Most people can't process something unless it happens to them."

"Presley isn't 'most people,'" Devon grumbled, but there was no point in getting into that part of her Keaton life with Raven. She still had bigger problems at hand. "So what'd you find?"

"The yacht crew. When we did the first check, the numbers added up. That's what the cops found that night, too. But when we matched the video with the numbers, one of the crewmembers didn't match his ID badge. It's all on our computer next time you come over to Reed's." She hesitated. "Didn't exactly expect to find you here."

"Ha. One set of friends wonders why I've gone surf-centric. And you guys don't think I'm beachy enough. Can't win, can I?"

Raven nudged Devon with her foot. "I'm going in. You want to be more beachy, try actually getting into the water at some point." She grabbed her surfboard and wrapped the Velcro strap around her ankle, then nodded to the parking lot. "Here's the surf king now. You know if you asked, he'd probably love to show you how to surf. Think on it."

Devon turned to see Bodhi stepping out of his blue Volkswagen camper, his own surfboard strapped to a roof rack. The door slammed shut, and Bodhi tucked his hands in the pocket of his hoodie, then turned to check out the water. He lifted his chin in a nod to Devon and Raven.

"You're not going in?" Devon called as he approached.

Bodhi arrived at Devon's boulder and sat down in the sand across from her. He squinted into the glare of the sun off the water. "Nah, the waves look a little small. I'll wait until they pick up a bit."

"Whatever," Raven said. She zipped her wetsuit up the back and jogged toward the ocean. Bodhi was silent as they watched Raven drop onto her board, paddling her way into the surf with ease.

"Where's Cleo?" Devon asked.

"Probably doing whatever she wants. We're not, like, hanging out anymore or anything, just so you know," he added quickly.

"At least one of you is keeping me in the loop," Devon muttered. "Cleo never said anything. Not that it matters."

Why would it matter? Why was Bodhi telling her this, anyway? It was none of her business. Although she did have to fight back a small smile. Cleo and Bodhi had always seemed like a poor match. But it wasn't because Devon was jealous or anything. She just figured Bodhi would be drawn to someone a little more grounded, a little less mega-yacht.

"It's not, like, weird or anything between us, but it probably wasn't a good call to hook up with a Keaton student," Bodhi clarified. "You know how word gets around."

Devon nodded, suddenly wanting to switch topics. "So Raven said you found a weird thing with the crew on the yacht? One of their IDs didn't match?"

"Yeah. One of the caterers, Isaac something . . . Isaac Green." Bodhi tugged at one of his own dreads, which hung loose around his shoulders, his blue eyes distant. "He called in sick that day. We found the note in their company emails. Don't ask us how; it's better you don't know. The point is, Isaac Green called in sick, but he also showed up to work that night."

Devon's stomach started to spin just at the memory of her slow-motion fall into the railing. That glimmer of the metal spyglass, twirling end over end and disappearing into the dark water. "You think that's our guy?" she breathed.

Bodhi shrugged again. "I have pictures to show you in case something rings a bell. You can come by the guest house whenever. I just keep thinking about what you were saying, that someone did this on purpose. And I keep coming back to the Hutchins family. They're the only ones that would have it in for you. But even Bill wouldn't get his hands dirty like this. With Eric's trial coming up, it just seems too obvious, even for them." Bodhi dug his hand into the sand and slowly lifted it up, letting the sand rain off. He smiled at the water. "She actually got a good one."

Devon turned to see Raven riding a wave and then flipping her board over the top of the small crest, dropping down again to paddle back out.

"Well, we know that Eric doesn't mind getting his hands dirty," Devon said. "I wouldn't put it past him to have orchestrated something like this. He has enough money at his disposal. Besides, he's been waiting out his trial at his parents' house in Pacific Heights. It's probably not the most restrictive situation."

Bodhi sniffed. "Yeah, that house arrest thing is totally cush. The guy commits murder, tries to hurt you, and he can still buy his way out of jail."

An idea began to worm its way into Devon's mind. "Do you think you can visit someone who's on house arrest?" she asked.

"Nah," Bodhi said with a laugh. "Not going to happen. I know where your head is at. You're not visiting Eric Hutchins."

She scooped sand onto her bare feet, covering them and then drawing an outline of where her foot would be. "But it kind of makes sense when you think about it. If someone is trying to kill me, why not visit the last person who tried to kill me?"

"No way. They'll never let you in to see him. You're a witness in the trial."

Devon finally met his gaze. "That's why you're going to help me."

CHAPTER 3

Phase one of the plan involved volunteering to be the "Ball Bitch."

The Keaton soccer team was playing Waldorf that Saturday in San Francisco, and being Ball Bitch meant Devon would be in charge of carrying a bag of soccer balls to and from the game with the team on the Keaton bus. "What good is self-directed gym if we can't help out our favorite teams?" she had asked Coach Duncan in the dining hall that morning. "Besides, school spirit always looks good on a college application. My extracurricular activities have suffered since . . . you know."

She hated playing the pity-over-Hutch's-death card, but extraordinary circumstances called for extraordinary measures. And however thin her logic, there *was* room on the bus. Plus, Coach Duncan needed the help, so he couldn't say no.

Once the game got started at the Waldorf campus—Presley

quickly put the Keaton team in a comfortable lead—Devon excused herself to find the nearest bathroom. Coach Duncan barely noticed her leaving the bench. Between clutching the stopwatch around his neck or chewing on the pencil he stored behind his ear, Devon knew he would be too distracted to keep track of how long she was gone.

Luckily Bodhi was right on time, his camper idling in the school parking lot just like they had planned. With one quick glance behind her to make sure no one was looking, Devon pried open the heavy passenger door. "Good timing," she said.

Bodhi turned the radio off. Devon realized she had never been in Bodhi's car before. Raven's beat-up Volvo, yes. Reed Hutchins's Range Rover, yes, but never Bodhi's camper.

"You still want to do this?" Bodhi asked. "We could just drive across the Golden Gate, get a bite at the marina. Or hang here until the game is over."

Devon knew what Bodhi was trying to do. She hadn't seen Eric since that night two months ago when he'd tried to slice open her wrist at the Palace. Luckily Devon's friends, Bodhi included, had been able to save her. But what if they hadn't been there?

Devon might not have met with Eric if she didn't know she had the support. Yet she did often wonder about that night. Would Eric really have killed her? She kept returning to Maya Dover: quiet, all business, the girl formerly just down the hall. Maya had gone out of her way to have an affair with Eric. Their families hated each other for reasons Devon still didn't understand. But Maya and Eric were having a baby, and from what Devon could tell, they really did care about each other. Maybe they even loved each other. This was the key to getting through to Eric. This was how she could humanize him—to herself included.

The brothers' grandfather, Reed, had told Devon that power and money have a way of poisoning men. Eric had killed his brother out of anger over his inheritance. She could almost believe how Eric's jealousy over Hutch had gotten the better of him. At one point Eric probably really did love Hutch, but the part of Eric that allowed him to cross that line, the part that said, *Do it,* was probably always in him too. And it was all the more reason to see Eric in person. If someone out there wanted Devon dead, she had to look Eric in the eye to know if it was him or not. She had to see if the evil within him had taken root and flourished.

"We're doing this," Devon said out loud, looking straight ahead.

"Well, you're lucky that you've got one awesome bodyguard." Bodhi pulled a black piece of fabric off his wrist and slipped it over his head. Devon smiled. There was something funny about watching Bodhi expertly pull his thick head of dreadlocked hair back in one simple move. It was almost . . . elegant. "Pacific Heights, here we come." He shifted the camper into reverse.

"The Keaton bus leaves in two hours. Think I'll be on it?" Devon asked.

"Done. No one will even know you were gone," Bodhi said with a wink.

PACIFIC HEIGHTS WAS SAID to have one of the best views in San Francisco. Devon had only driven through it before; no one she knew from home was exactly Pacific Heights material. But when Bodhi pulled up across the street from the Hutchins family home, Devon wondered if the Hutchins family might have *the* best view in the city. Perfectly situated at the top of a steep hill, the three-story villa—there was nothing else to call it—overlooked the Golden Gate Bridge and the San Francisco Bay, across the water to Mill Valley. The pink color of the stone even somehow avoided looking like a Pepto Bismol catastrophe—but regal and elegant.

"Let me do the talking," Bodhi said, locking the front door to the VW. He wiped his hands on his navy-blue Carhartt pants.

Devon looked down at her Keaton hoodie, jeans, and Converse—then at Bodhi's grubby pants, flannel shirt, and Vans. Damn, she hadn't thought that part through. Keaton-casual does not apply well to the outside world. Why did she always forget that? The Hutchins family probably had a separate entrance for their service staff, and Devon was pretty sure she and Bodhi looked more suited to that than they did to sit down for tea with Mitzi. Bodhi reapplied his headband to little effect. His bleached-blond dreads stuck out from the back of his head like porcupine quills. There was definitely no way tea would be offered.

Summoning her courage, Devon trailed him up the front steps. The doorbell echoed when he pushed it.

Silence.

She looked around for signs of Eric's house arrest. Shouldn't there be sensors to note the boundaries of the house? Maybe Devon was confusing house arrest with an electric dog collar. The ornate stone lions standing guard at the foot of the stairwell seemed appropriate, like Devon was there to visit a prisoner in ancient Rome.

Bodhi pressed the doorbell again.

"Coming!" Eric's muffled voice shouted.

When he answered the door, barefoot in jeans and a plain white T-shirt, he didn't seem like much of a prisoner. His chin-length hair had gotten longer and hung just above his shoulders, and he seemed to be growing a beard. His eyes narrowed, and he sighed heavily. "You two. What now?"

Bodhi stroked his chin. "Nice little grow going on there. You quit shaving? Mine just comes in in patches."

Eric just glared at him. "Why did you bring her here? After everything this family has done for you?"

"I actually need to ask you something," Devon said. "It was my idea."

"Oh, yeah? Well, ask away, little Keaton. Ask away." Eric rubbed his shoulder against the doorframe, his eyes only on Bodhi.

"Who's trying to kill me?"

Eric laughed and turned to her. "Always full of surprises. You came here to ask me that?"

Bodhi stepped forward. "Someone attacked her on New Year's Eve," he said in his mellowest voice. "At a yacht party. She thinks you might be helpful in figuring out who it was. We can go. I figured you didn't know anything." He shoved his hands in his pockets and started to turn away.

Eric laughed again, a bitter cackle. "This is the most entertainment I've had in weeks. Come on in. I wanna hear more about this conspiracy theory of yours." He made a sweeping gesture and stepped aside.

As Devon squeezed past Bodhi at the door, he mumbled, "I'm not letting you out of my sight." His hand grazed the small of her back. Devon sneaked him a grateful smile. Bodhi was bigger than Eric—bigger, and in the end, probably tougher.

Whoa, Devon thought, taking in the house. It was like walking into a *Vanity Fair* spread. A long staircase with a wooden banister sloped to the second floor in a relaxed curve. A wide chandelier hung from the two-story ceiling in a stylish array of crystal, metal, and light. Eric escorted them down the hallway to the living room. Or maybe it was a sitting room? A den? A library? What sort of terms did people like this use for their endless museum-quality assemblages of stiff sofas and carpets and sculpture?

"So it's open season on Devon, is it?" Eric said with a smile as he sat down in a large wingback chair. "Forgive me if I find that a little funny."

Devon felt her heartbeat quicken. She sat across from him. Bodhi remained standing. "You think someone trying to kill me is funny?" she demanded. "You must be more of a sociopath than I originally thought."

Eric's smile dropped. "You're going to testify against me in the trial, aren't you? So yeah, I've thought about how nice it would be if you didn't exist, but it's not like I did anything about it. I'm already in deep enough shit as it is." He leaned back and crossed his ankle over his knee. It was impossible to ignore the gray plastic ankle bracelet with a small green light. Eric noticed her stare as she quickly tried to look elsewhere. "You wanna get a good look? This is what it looks like when your future gets flushed down the toilet."

Bodhi drummed his fingers against his thigh. He finally sat beside Devon. "Doesn't look too bad from where I sit."

"Mr. Hutchins?" a woman's voice called.

Devon and Bodhi turned. So they weren't alone in the house. That was reassuring. Her fists unclenched at her sides.

"I thought you and your guests might like something to drink." A thirty-ish Hispanic woman, fashionably dressed, entered the room, carrying a tray of soda, a silver ice bucket, and crystal tumblers. She placed the tray on the coffee table. Devon and Bodhi smiled and thanked her, while Eric pressed his lips together and looked out the window until she was gone.

"I'm sorry," Devon said. "You were saying something about this being a horrible way to live?"

Bodhi gave her a slight smile.

"Look," Eric said, ignoring the drinks. "I don't know who or what happened to you on that boat. I have enough going on here. I am not going to complicate my situation. I've been kicked out of Stanford, and I'll never get into med school now. And if for some reason I don't spend the rest of my life in jail, I'll forever be labeled a felon. You think that goes over well in job interviews? I'm screwed, Devon. Completely screwed."

"Yeah, but at least you're not dead, which is more than Hutch can say," Devon heard herself hiss.

"She didn't mean that," Bodhi said quickly. "Sorry, we came here for your help, not to point fingers." He bumped her knee with his own. It was her cue.

Devon took a second to collect herself. How dare Eric sit here and have the gall to complain about his life when he'd taken Hutch's from him?

"Bodhi's right. I'm sorry." She forced the words out of her mouth. "We came here for your help. I shouldn't have said that. Sorry." She couldn't believe she was actually apologizing to Eric of all people, but it was the only way.

"Guess I'm going to have to get used to people hating me," Eric said quietly. It was the first time Devon had seen him show the faintest hint of remorse. If there was a caring human underneath the horrible rich boy persona Eric had so carefully cultivated, now was the time to find him.

"Have you heard anything from Maya?" Devon asked. "About the baby?"

When Eric looked up at her, she saw fear. Maya *was* his humanity; she knew it then. She and that baby were his salvation, even if he couldn't participate in their lives. "They won't let me talk to her. Her parents sent her somewhere to have the baby. Why? What have you heard? She's okay, isn't she?"

Devon shook her head. "I haven't heard anything. I saw her mom moving her out of her dorm room, but that was it. I guess she's not coming back to Keaton, that's for sure." She hoped what she was about to suggest wasn't a terrible idea. "I could try to find out for you. Where she is. See if you can email her or something. I mean, only if you think it would help her. I don't want to interfere."

"Why would you do that for me?" Eric asked. His tone was soft now.

"Yeah, why *would* you do that?" Bodhi demanded, his tone the opposite.

Devon shrugged. "Because Maya's pregnant and she's been pulled from school. She's probably lonely and afraid. And if you still care about her, maybe she'd like to know that. I would, if I was in her shoes."

Eric dropped his head and let out a long sigh before he spoke again. "If you can do that, I'd . . . I don't know, Devon. If you can get me an email that works for her? A phone? An address? I'll send freakin' smoke signals if I have to, I just don't know where. That'd be amazing. Thank you."

Bodhi looked at his watch and shoved it in front of Devon. Thirty-five minutes until the Keaton bus would leave Waldorf. "Hate to cut this short, but we've got to get going," he said.

Devon took a deep breath and stood.

Eric looked between them and nodded. "Yeah, okay." He stood up, too. "You know, you're actually the only people who've visited me. Not sure what that says about my friends, but . . . thanks." He started to walk them back down the long hallway. "Devon, if I knew anything about who attacked you on some boat, I would tell you. I don't know who it would be or why. You were just trying to do the right thing by Hutch. I can't hold that against you."

Devon couldn't bring herself to look him again. "Thanks, I think."

"You know, we knew about you before Keaton. Before Hutch even started."

She froze in midstep. "What? How?"

Eric snickered as he opened the front door. The sudden bright sunlight burned Devon's eyes. "You really don't know, do you?" he asked. "You know, I don't think I ever really believed that you *didn't* know until this moment. I thought you were just playing the ignorant poor girl this whole time. Who do you think pays for your scholarship?"

She whirled to face him, but he was already closing the door behind them. "It's a trust. Some trust set up for Keaton kids that need financial aid. Isn't it?"

"Nosy in all the wrong places, as always . . ."

"Wait. Who set up the trust?" Devon demanded.

"I'd look a little deeper into that one if I were you."

The door slammed shut.

CHAPTER 4

The bus ride back to school seemed like an eternity. Devon tried calling her mom, then texting her, but there was no reply. *She must be working*, Devon reasoned. When her mom was at the hospital, all bets were off where trying to get hold of her was concerned.

Bodhi had promised to call Raven on his way back to Reed's to get a jump-start on looking up the scholarship trust. Alone in one of the rear seats, Devon stared at her phone, willing the answers to arrive. She couldn't shake Eric's words. *We knew about you before Keaton.* How? Why did he believe she was putting on an act? She *was* an ignorant poor girl. Well, not *poor* . . . but definitely not rich enough to pay for Keaton without help. Was Hutch's and Eric's father on a board or something that gave Eric an early look at the incoming scholarship students? She knew there were the basic admissions and financial aid conversations, but why would Bill Hutchins be involved in those? Sure, he donated heavily to the school, but that didn't give him the right to decide who gets to attend Keaton, did it?

Devon's mind whirled. The school had granted her mom financial aid to supplement her tuition fees. It was that simple as far as she'd always known. Her mom worked as a nurse at the Trinity Hospital in Berkeley, so *supplement* was really a generous way of saying: *We think you're a good enough student to cover your ass.* Without that scholarship, there was no way Devon would be attending Keaton.

Up until now, she'd believed what she'd been told, that the money came from a general alumni trust. When alumni donated to the school, they could specify that their money should go to certain causes. There was no single person taking credit for that trust. But Eric had asked her, *Who do you think pays for your scholarship?* Was he implying that there *was* a single, anonymous person paying for Devon specifically? If so, why? And why would that information be withheld from her or her mom? Wouldn't that person want it known?

Devon glanced out the window as the bus wound its way down Highway 1 into Monte Vista, the Pacific Ocean rolling against the cliffs below. The farther they got from San Francisco, the more the pine trees and redwoods thickened on the hillside.

"Where there's money, there are breadcrumbs leading to that money."

That's what Bodhi had said before he dropped her back off at the game. She closed her eyes and tried to keep the panic at bay. If anyone could find her anonymous donor, Bodhi and Raven could. She said a silent prayer that their discovery wouldn't lead right back to the Hutchins family. If they were the ones who had been paying for her scholarship this whole time . . .

Devon couldn't finish the thought. Hutch would have known. He would have told her, wouldn't he? Or even worse, if he'd known and had pitied her . . . And then for Devon to be the one that got Eric's confession about Hutch on camera? That family must hate her. But that was the question. Did they hate her enough to want her dead?

The bus shuddered as it shifted gears to begin the climb up the hillside from Monte Vista to Keaton. She couldn't face the thought of Saturday night stuck on the hill. While she'd been preoccupied with her meeting with Eric, most students had arranged for overnights off campus, or even just a chaperoned trip into Santa Cruz. Raven and Bodhi could help her sneak away for a few hours after dinner sign-in.

She sent Raven a text. Must escape tonight. Pick me up at 7? Fire road.

Raven responded quickly. kk :p

BY SEVEN IT WAS sufficiently dark on the hillside for Devon to sneak unseen along the hidden trail below Bay House. She shivered in the salty midwinter ocean breeze. Last time she'd gone down this trail, it had been to meet Eric Hutchins. Farther down the hill was the Palace, where Eric had given his only brother a fatal dose of Oxycontin. But right now she only hoped that there weren't any rogue students sneaking a smoke or a drink. The dirt road that connected the Keaton hillside to the Hutchinses' hillside was still a secret that Devon hoped the Keaton faculty wouldn't think to block off. Since Hutch's death, it had remained her own little private escape route, the perfect way to steal a few hours from the constant chaos of her dorm.

The familiar black Range Rover idled on the path up ahead. Devon picked up her pace with a last glance at the lights of Bay House. In the car, the green glow of dashboard lights lit up Raven's silhouette.

"You cool?" Raven asked when Devon opened the passenger door.

The interior light lit up the car, making Devon wince. Bad move; somebody would be able to see that. She got in and quickly shut the door.

"Now I am," she said. She let out a long breath. Even the promise of getting off campus made her more relaxed. "Let's go."

"Bodhi said today was kind of a doozy," Raven said. She scrunched up one side of her face. "Sorry, but the house is a little nutty, gotta warn you. Probably not quite the peace you were hoping for."

Headlights off, she cautiously backed down the incline until the road was wide enough for her to turn around. Devon squinted as her eyes adjusted, taking in the black grapevines cutting across the mountain like a line of stitches. Raven downshifted as the car dug into the bumpy hillside climbing toward Reed's property, its wheels kicking up the loose dirt behind them.

"Is the family still ganging up on Grandpa Reed?" Devon asked. She gripped her seat as the car trudged forward in giant hiccups up the hill like an aging roller coaster. The top of the hill came into view, and Devon could make out the first of the lights lining Reed's driveway.

Raven gave the car one last burst of gas. It revved in place for a second before kicking into gear and lurching forward over the crest and onto the driveway in front of Reed's guesthouse, where Raven's beat-up Volvo and Bodhi's VW van were parked. Farther up the driveway, Devon glimpsed a silver Audi sports car. Something that fancy probably cost six figures.

"Yeah, ol' Billy Boy is here," Raven said, catching Devon's squint. "He came to yell at Reed about something else he doesn't care about. It's been a real chill evening." She smiled and shook her head. "Come on in. Bodhi's waiting."

"Thanks. And hey, thanks for the bailout. If I stayed on campus, I was going to go nuts researching my scholarship thing."

"So you came *here* to research your scholarship thing," Raven said with a playful smirk. She pulled the keys from the ignition. "We know why you love us."

Reed Hutchins's guesthouse had become Raven's and Bodhi's full-time residence since Reed asked them to move in after Hutch died. Devon still didn't know the whole story with the Elliot siblings' father, but they were clearly relieved to be out of his house and have the luxury of Reed's high-end computers and desk space available. Plus, Reed had made it very clear that he was both impressed with and fascinated by what they could find with their hacking skills.

Devon walked into the kitchen to find Bodhi pulling a burrito out of the microwave. "Ah, formal dinner tonight, I see," she said.

"It's always formal dinner *chez* Elliot." Bodhi pulled a stool away from the counter for Devon. "What can I get you, mademoiselle? Our specials tonight are pepperoni Hot Pockets or bean-and-cheese burritos. Either of which could be ready for you in a cool minute and thirty seconds." Bodhi bit into his burrito and quickly waved his hand in front of his mouth. "Ahhht. Oooh ahhht," he managed to say.

"Huh. So that's what a real genius looks like." Devon laughed as Bodhi hopped from foot to foot, frantically chewing. "How illuminating."

"Okay, now I'm actually hungry," Raven said. She opened the refrigerator first (empty), then opened the freezer, which was packed with microwave meals for days. She pulled out a stack of mini-pizzas. "Dev, want one? Actually cooked in the oven?"

"Sure, thanks." Devon realized she was actually hungry, too. She sat down at the counter. Bodhi slid a laptop in front of her.

"Here, we found you this." He opened up a file labeled *Marina Gourmet*. "So this was the list of waiters and bartenders hired by the catering company. Most of them have worked with the company before at other events."

"Who knew caterers made such good money?" Raven commented across the room. "Like, twenty-five bucks an hour."

"I'll keep that in mind when I'm looking for a summer job." Devon scooted closer to Bodhi. "What else did you find?"

"Okay, we've got who worked the event on the yacht. Everyone has to check in with the manager and swipe their ID cards. There were fifteen waiters, all checked in that evening. Here's the picture of Isaac Green from his company card." Bodhi opened an image of a regular-looking guy—brown curly hair, nice smile, but forgettable. "And here's who showed up to work that night with Isaac Green's ID."

The next image felt like a punch in the gut to Devon. The dimples . . . that was all she needed to see. They had pulled a picture of Cleo's waiter carrying a tray of champagne flutes from one of the security cameras.

"He introduced himself to me as Eli," Devon said.

Raven chuckled. "What an idiot. Why would he do that?"

Bodhi arched his eyebrows at his sister. "He hit Devon on the back of the head with a blunt instrument with the hope that she might fall off the yacht and drown. But why would he introduce himself as the wrong name? *That's* what you want to know?"

Raven shrugged. "Yeah. That's what I want to know. Think about it. Why would someone, probably a professional that has most likely been hired to carry out this insane job, make such a huge mistake?"

"Maybe he's not that good?" Devon mumbled, more to herself than anyone else in the room. She stared at the black-and-white image. The short brown hair, the dimples set in a fixed smile as he walked, but his eyes looking off to the side . . . it appeared he was already surveying the scene. Raven had a point. Before New Year's Eve, Devon had never seen him before in her life. Not that this was a prerequisite for attacking her, but it was hard to believe that this twenty-something guy woke up that morning and decided to steal someone's identity, work as a waiter at a yacht party, and then randomly pick Devon to assault with a metal spyglass. *Who* attacked her wasn't really the question here. *Why* would someone attack her was the scarier thought to consider.

Devon looked up from the computer at Bodhi and Raven, who were watching her reaction. "Anyone could be Isaac Green, or Eli, whatever his name is," she said. "He's not the point. Someone else is behind this, and I have a feeling we won't be able to find them until we know *why* they want me dead."

Neither Bodhi nor Raven spoke.

The crack of an intercom startled the three of them. "Raven? Bodhi?" a woman's voice blared. "Is Devon there with you?"

Raven and Bodhi scowled at each other.

"We know you're there," the woman said. "Your cars are in the driveway."

Bodhi sighed and went to the small cream-colored panel near the door. He leaned in and pressed a button, his face lit up in a big phony smile. "Yes, Priscilla. We're all here."

"Can you send Devon up to the house? Mr. Hutchins would like to speak with her. And Bodhi, I can hear your sarcasm from here."

Bodhi rolled his eyes.

"What's going on?" Devon whispered to Raven.

Raven and Bodhi shared another glance, this one more troubled. Raven twisted her lips into a crooked line. "Reed's gotten worse. He's got a full-time nursing staff up there. Refuses to check into a hospital. That's Priscilla; she's been running things."

"And she makes sure we know it," Bodhi added. "Come on, I'll walk you up."

Devon followed him back into the cold of the front courtyard, where she caught a whiff of basil and rosemary bushes in the wine-barrels-turned-planters outside the front door. Above, the moon was in that awkward stage between full and half, but the light was bright enough to make the white flowers on the walk up the driveway glow. It was so peaceful here—aside from whoever this Priscilla woman was—that the Hutchins compound seemed farther away than ever from Keaton.

"So do you think Eric has enough motive to hire someone to go on the boat?" Bodhi asked quietly.

Devon shook her head. "Doesn't fit somehow, you know? I know he hates me for catching him, which is fine, but *kill* me? He's got too much else on his mind. Besides, he's got too big of an ego to let someone else do something that big for him. He's a total control freak." Devon paused. "I mean, that's my opinion, at least. What do you think?"

Bodhi looked over at her before answering. "I don't think this is about Hutch. I think we're not seeing the whole picture." He bit his lip, allowing his dreads to fall in front of his face for a moment before brushing them back. "Just so you know, Reed doesn't know about any of this. He's got enough to deal with."

"I . . . I'm sorry, Bodhi," Devon murmured. She reached out and squeezed his hand. They were almost at the front door, and she realized she didn't know what she was about to walk in to. She slowed until they were standing at the steps below the front door. "He's really bad?"

Bodhi nodded but couldn't make eye contact with Devon. She suddenly felt like a jerk. All of this obsessing about one incident, and here were Bodhi and Raven, watching as their stand-in parent was flirting with Death. Hell, flirting was putting it mildly. Reed was *in a relationship* with Death.

Devon realized she and Bodhi were still holding hands. She gave him another squeeze. "Hey, you know I'm here for you guys, too. It doesn't always have to be the other way around."

"Thanks, but you know what? Dealing with your stuff is just way more fun than this." Bodhi nodded toward the house looming above them, but held on to her hand for a few more seconds. "Shall we?"

CHAPTER 5

Before Devon had made it halfway across the front hall, she heard yelling. Bodhi ducked into the shadow behind the archway leading into the living room and put a finger to his lips.

"There are still treatments you haven't tried yet!" came a man's voice.

Devon couldn't recognize it. He wasn't Reed; this guy was too healthy, too dominant. But who would have the gall to yell at a dying man? She leaned forward and glimpsed the tightly cropped gray hair of Bill Hutchins—Reed's son and Hutch's father. He was bent over someone. "We've got some good options in R&D, and that's not even including what Dover's got. His company has a cancer-research division twice the size of ours. Why don't you call Edward? You know he'd help if you would just let him—"

"I will have nothing to do with that man, and you know it."

Devon cringed at the sound of Reed's voice. It was calm and firm, but fragile. The words were like sandpaper, followed by a few wheezing breaths.

"Dad, listen to me." Bill softened his tone. "We've got to make peace with them. It's the only way to move forward. We're losing money holding out for no good reason, and you know it."

Reed cleared his throat. "Not everything in life is always about money, William. I thought I raised you better than that. If you don't listen to me now, you're going to learn that the hard way later. Do not trust Edward Dover . . ." The rest was lost in a fit of coughing.

Devon winced at the sound, so strained and sickly.

More wheezing breaths, followed by the slurp of a straw in a cup. "Priscilla!"

"That's it!" Bill spat. His footsteps pounded toward Devon's hiding place.

She and Bodhi looked at each other, wide-eyed. Should they say something before being discovered? Bodhi leaned forward, about to take the first step, when a short nurse rounded the corner in front of them—in pink scrubs, squeaky white tennis shoes with pink laces, and her hair neatly pulled back into a long braid. She stopped short. Then she drew in a sharp breath and frowned at Bodhi, her eyes flashing at Devon. Shaking her head, she continued into the living room.

"Priscilla, there you are," Reed croaked.

Bodhi hesitated another few seconds before he stepped out of the shadows with Devon. Bill turned at the sound. His eyes narrowed.

Was that glare aimed at Bodhi or her?

"Do you need to get up, Mr. Hutchins?" Priscilla went straight to Reed's side.

Devon tried to smile at Reed across the room. Her heart squeezed.

Reed was propped up in a large hospital bed made up with dark-green-and-red plaid flannel sheets, with a thick tan blanket draped across his legs. The sleeves of his red robe were slightly rolled up to reveal his thin wrists. A square bandage across the top of his palm held an IV in place, with the plastic line extending up into a clear bag of fluid hanging by the top of the bed. He'd lost a lot of weight and color since the last time she'd seen him. The skin over his bones was practically translucent.

"The chair, please, Priscilla. I have company," Reed said with a kind smile. "Bill, I expect I'll hear from you tomorrow."

Bill grunted and turned to leave. He glared at Devon—definitely at her this time—as he crossed the room to the front door. Moments later, the door slammed behind him, followed by the purr of his Audi's engine.

"We're not interrupting, right?" Bodhi asked. He sat at the foot of Reed's bed. "Priscilla said you wanted to see Devon."

"Of course I do. Devon, welcome to the Hospital Hutchins." Reed's arm flailed in small circles as he tried to look behind him. Priscilla was returning with a wheelchair. "Bodhi, maybe you could help us here."

Bodhi patted Reed's leg and used the remote control attached to the metal handrail to move the bed into a more upright position. Reed smiled at Devon and rolled his eyes. "I spend most of my day just waiting around on this bed." Gripping Bodhi's arm with one arm and firmly wrapping the other around the handrail, he hoisted himself into the wheelchair. He trembled with the effort.

Priscilla dropped the foot pedals and tucked a blanket across his lap. "Now you're off to the races, Mr. Hutchins."

"Devon, will you push me to my office?" Reed wheezed.

She hesitated; she'd never pushed anyone in a wheelchair before. Bodhi nodded, giving her the okay.

"If you want, yeah—I mean, yes, of course." Priscilla turned the wheelchair around for her and stepped aside for Devon to take the handles. "This way?" she asked as she started pushing Reed down the hall.

"Onward, ho!" Reed clucked, like he was spurring a horse. Devon had to give him credit; the guy never lost his sense of humor.

The inside of his office was exactly what Devon imagined it would be: softly lit, wood-paneled like everything else in the cabin, a wall of bookshelves from floor to ceiling. The other wall was a patchwork of cupboards and shelves.

"Sorry about Bill," Reed said as Devon pushed him deeper into the office. He pointed a skeletal finger at the cupboard across the room. Devon wheeled him in that direction. "Still hasn't come to terms with death, I suppose. Mine or Jason's. That's the problem with scientists today. Instead of learning from death, they want to cheat it. Usually not for anyone's good but their own." He drew a deep gasping breath and opened a lower door.

Devon took on a seat on a nearby chair to face him. "You sound pretty Zen about everything," she murmured, unable to keep the awe from her voice. His eyes were rheumy and seemed to have shrunken in their sockets.

He pulled a cracked leather-bound book from the cupboard and placed it on the nearby desk. His gnarled fingers remained draped over the cover. "I think it's because this isn't about me anymore. After all these years, I'm ready to stop fighting. My body wants to give up; who am I to fight it? But Devon, that's why I wanted to speak to you. What happens after I'm gone is what concerns me most." He slid the book toward her. "You'll need this to get up to speed on everything."

She picked it up, the leather brittle in her hands, the pages yellowed with who-knew-how-many years. Clearly this book was much older than she was, probably older than Reed himself. Which begged the question: why would she need it to get up to speed?

"For the land," he wheezed, reading the confusion on her face.

She shook her head. "I don't understand . . ."

"You'll need to know how all of this began, how it involves me and Francis Keaton and Edward Dover. The three trees of this mountain. Once I'm gone, you'll need to know what we're protecting and what you're going to have to fight for."

Devon flipped through the first few pages. It was mostly handwriting, like a diary, mixed with pages and pages of formulas and diagrams. "Are you sure you didn't mean for Raven or Bodhi to read this?" she asked, baffled. "They probably understand the science better than I do."

"No," Reed said. He slapped a hand on top of the desk and leaned forward in his chair. His eyes focused intensely on Devon's. The red-tinged whites threatened to overtake his sky-blue pupils. "This is for *you*. You need to know what they'll want from you." His breathing caught, and he broke into a coughing fit. He gasped for air while Devon watched, too panicked to move. Reed's eye's fluttered. *Oh, God, please don't die right here.* She reached for the door as Priscilla burst inside with an oxygen tank apparatus, complete with a mask and plastic hoses.

The nurse gave Devon a polite yet stern push against the wall. Without hesitation, she strapped a plastic mouthpiece onto Reed's face. His breath fogged up the clear plastic in alternating breaths. Priscilla studied him as she hooked the tank to the back of his chair. His eyes seemed to regain their focus; they sought out Devon across the room. He pulled the mask low and croaked, "Take the diary. You'll need it to follow our footsteps. Follow our footsteps, Devon. Follow them."

Devon's eyes flitted to Priscilla. Reed subtly shook his head as if to say, *Don't worry about her.* Her legs shaky, she crossed the room. How could she be so afraid in the face of such bravery? But she knew it was more than fear of losing yet another Hutchins; it was fear of what she didn't understand. Something about Reed's instructions felt so final.

Priscilla gripped the handles on the wheelchair and started to push Reed out of the office. His breath still fogged up the oxygen mask, but his eyes never left Devon.

Before she had time to wonder if it was a good idea or even safe, she took Reed's hand in between hers and knelt down, eye level with the ailing old man. "Thank you. For trusting me with this."

Reed's eyes blinked slow, his silent acknowledgment. She kissed his cheek, his onion-paper-y skin soft against her lips. He pulled his mask down one more time. "I'm trusting you with a lot more than just the book," he whispered. "It's your turn now, Devon. I'll tell Hutch everything's in good hands." He winked at her as Priscilla wheeled him out of the office.

"Mr. Hutchins needs his rest now," Priscilla said to Devon over her shoulder.

Devon watched Reed roll down the dark hallway. She'd never believed in premonition; it defied everything she believed about the realities of human nature, not to mention reality itself. Yet she knew for certain that this would be the last time she saw him. It had been written in his eyes.

SKIMMING THROUGH REED'S DIARY while eating pizza with Raven and Bodhi in the guesthouse somehow felt wrong. The diary deserved Devon's full attention; it was a part of Reed, something sacred. But of course Raven wouldn't let Devon return to school without finishing their interrupted microwave feast, so Devon quietly tucked the book into her backpack. Bodhi stayed glued to his computer, looking into Isaac Green and the mysterious Eli.

"He lives in the Mission District in the city. Takes a few classes at SFCC. And according to his Facebook page, he's currently single."

Devon felt his eyes on her across the room. Suddenly self-conscious, she chose to stay focused on Raven.

"Well, that answers everything, then," Raven said with a wink. She took another bite of her mini-pizza and stretched a piece of cheese as long as it could go between her mouth and the pizza slice.

"So we just track down this Isaac Green in the Mission District?" Devon asked. Even as she posed the question, she thought of what Presley said at the beach. Did Devon really go out of her way to find trouble? Could she choose not to dig deeper? It would be so easy to let this go and move on, wouldn't it? Unless, of course, her attacker meant to kill her and wanted to finish a botched job . . .

"522 Dolores Street. Apartment 4A to be specific," Bodhi added.

"So we just go pay a visit to our good friend Isaac, ask him why someone else showed up to work with his ID that night?" Devon added. "That's it, right?"

Raven tossed her pizza crust onto her plate. "Have we ruled out the possibility that our friend Isaac—which, by the way, I totally think we should call him from now on—maybe didn't know about his ID being used? He could actually have no idea what happened."

"But his ID was scanned at the yacht," Devon said. Raven and Bodhi looked at each other and shrugged. "What? You think someone made that ID?"

"It wouldn't be that hard to do." Bodhi grinned slyly. "I mean, we could do it."

"Yeah, but you guys are . . . you," Devon said. "As hard to believe as it may be, not everyone has your superpowers."

"Don't they?" Raven asked with a raised eyebrow and a certain smirk reserved for her especially clever moments. "Okay, so there is still the possibility that our friend Isaac had no involvement with said yacht incident. You know we're gonna have to actually get an answer now—for Isaac's sake, too."

"Wait, what time is it?" Devon checked her phone. 9:50. "Damn, curfew is in ten minutes."

Bodhi stood up. "Maybe there's another soccer game in the city? Or next week, you take a weekend away over here?"

Raven began lacing up her high-tops. "Yeah, we can totally forge Reed's signature to get you over here."

"I'll take her," Bodhi said.

Devon threw her bag over a shoulder. The diary dug into her back, reminding her that it wanted to be read. She turned to Raven.

"No one else thinks this is weird or stalker-y of me, right? I mean, you guys don't have to get involved in all this. I know you've got enough going on with Reed being sick and all."

Raven rolled her eyes. "Hey, you're not crazy. Don't let your cohorts in the bubble on the hill let you think otherwise. We'll keep looking into this thing until we find the answers we want."

"Besides, there's nothing we can do for Reed now except to live in this house," Bodhi said quietly. He jangled the car keys in his hands. "Come on, you don't want to get in trouble."

Devon dashed forward and hugged Raven. "Thanks. The bubble can make you forget what's real sometimes."

"No shit," Raven murmured, squeezing back. "Night, Dev."

BODHI WAS QUIET IN the bumpy car ride back over the hill. The moon was so bright he didn't need to turn the lights on—not that he would have risked getting spotted, anyway. She knew that he wanted to keep this road off anyone else's radar as much as she did.

"Doesn't Reed actually own this hill?" Devon asked, watching the lights from the Keaton dorms grow closer, a deceptive warm campfire-like glow that promised comfort before the whole place went into full lockdown mode.

Bodhi considered the question for a moment. "I think there's a line here that divides the property. Hutchins and Keaton. Like an actual *line*. But Keaton and Reed were buddies all those years, so who knows? Maybe it was just a gentleman's handshake about the whole thing." Bodhi downshifted as the car crept up the slope below Bay House. The clock on the dashboard read 9:56. Devon would have to run to slip inside before curfew. Or sprint, more like it. Ms. Hadden was on dorm duty, and she purposely locked all the side doors in the building so there was only one way to get inside. She would be firmly parked at the main entrance with her clipboard in hand, checking each girl off her list as they filed in for the night. A faux-blonde jail warden in a Lacoste sweater.

The car lurched to a stop.

"Thanks for the ride," Devon said. She opened the door.

"I really don't think you're crazy," Bodhi said. "I wouldn't let anyone hurt you. You should know that. I mean . . . it means a lot to us that you're so concerned about Reed. But this research stuff, I want to—we want to do it."

"Um, thanks. That's good to know." Her voice sounded funny in her ears. Bodhi was staring at her with a strange intensity.

Before Devon understood what was happening, he had leaned across the center console and reached for her. With a hand on the back of her neck, he pulled Devon toward him and kissed her. A soft kiss at first, as if testing the waters. His dreadlocks brushed her cheeks; she was conscious of how they felt so much softer than how they looked. Then another, longer kiss, his fingers threaded through her hair, giving it a slow tug. He pulled away.

"I've thought about doing that for weeks," he whispered.

Devon glanced at the dashboard: 9:58.

Her heart thumped. Shit, I gotta go." She grabbed her backpack and jumped out of the car. Her lips were still warm and tingling from the kiss. She took a few steps but caught herself before going further. "Bodhi?"

He leaned out his window. His eyes glittered in the moonlight. He was smiling, but there was sadness there.

"I'm glad you did," she said.

His smile brightened. "Night, Devon."

"You, too." Devon turned and dashed up the hillside, her own smile as wide as the distance to her waiting dorm.

CHAPTER 6

The phone woke Devon the next morning. She had been dreaming about surfing . . . or rather, sitting on a surfboard in the ocean while the waves bobbed around her. The metal spyglass from the yacht floated nearby, but no matter how hard she paddled and kicked, she couldn't reach it. The ringing merged with the purr and snarl of the waves, growing louder and louder until it finally pulled her out of sleep.

"Hi, Mom." She groaned and slumped back into her pillow.

"Morning, sunshine. Sorry to wake you." Devon could hear her mom rustling through the kitchen at home. A cupboard slammed; the coffee machine beeped.

"Extra-strong brew?" Devon asked.

"Mmmm, you know the morning drill. Gotta fuel up for those fourteen-hour shifts." More cupboards slamming, plastic rustling.

"Listen, hon. Sorry I didn't call you back until now. You said something in your text about your scholarship?"

"Yeah, ummm." Devon took a deep breath. She needed some oxygen to get her brain running at capacity. And this was a tricky situation. She obviously couldn't tell her mom that she'd visited Hutch's murderer brother. But what was the best way to clue in her mom on the cryptic information Eric had divulged?

"I wanted to write a thank-you note or something to the people that help with my scholarship. You don't know anything about them, do you?"

"I know about as much as you do, hon," her mom said matter-of-factly. "It's a trust or something set up by the alumni association."

"Just one alum? Or a bunch? Wouldn't their names be listed somewhere?"

"I don't know. Maybe it's one of the truly generous people left in the world, someone who doesn't need to be recognized for their generosity. Why the sudden interest now? You never mentioned this before."

"So it's one alum who's responsible for the scholarship," Devon pressed.

"Honey, what's this about?" her mother asked. The puttering around the kitchen had stopped. There was dead silence on the other end.

Devon swallowed. "I don't know. I guess it's like how adopted kids suddenly decide they want to find their real parents, you know? Thinking about college and knowing I'll be leaving eventually, and how my whole Keaton experience being due to someone else's generosity and stuff." She closed her mouth. She was babbling.

Her mom sighed. "Hmm, I never thought of it that way." She took a sip of coffee, apparently placated. "I'm sure if you wrote a note to the administration, the school would make sure it went to the right person."

"Yeah, I could do that." Devon closed her eyes. If her worst fear was true, that her scholarship was paid for by the Hutchins family, then writing a letter of thanks to them wouldn't just be offensive, it would be plain stupid. *Thanks for my education. Oh, and sorry about exposing that your son murdered your other son over money. Cheers!* No way.

"Hey, you ever hear of the Hutchins family?" she heard herself ask. "I mean, before everything happened with Hutch?"

The movement on the other end came to another standstill. Devon's mom's voice was quieter now, more measured. "I feel so horrible for those poor parents. No parent should have to go through that."

"So you don't think they could secretly be super generous?"

"Why would you ask that? You think they're connected to your scholarship? Devon, I'm not sure I like where you're going with this—"

"I only want to find out if they're really generous," Devon said defensively, and mostly to herself. "I don't think that's a terrible thing to be accused of."

A long sigh, and longer silence on the other end. "I've got to get to work." Her mother's voice was sharp now, tired. "Whoever provided your scholarship chose to remain anonymous, and we have to respect that choice. So please, let's just be grateful for someone's generosity and drop it. If you want to write a letter for the school, I'm sure they'll get it to the right person."

"Or people. Like you said, you don't know it's just one person—"

"It's not our business, Devon."

"This is my forty-thousand-dollar-a-year education. How is that not my business? Why are you being so weird about this?"

There was a sharp rattle; her mother must have put down her mug extra hard on the counter. "You haven't listened to a word I've said. I can hear you getting worked up. That's not what we need."

"We? Are we speaking in the royal 'we' now?"

"Devon, I have to go. Enjoy your Sunday. I love you, sunshine."

"*We* love you, too, Mom. Bye." She hung up and closed her eyes again.

Was her mom mad at her? She seemed touchy about the questions, or could Devon have been imagining that? No, her mom had definitely seemed off. Better question: Was her own mother sick of Devon's questions? Or worse, was her mom keeping a secret from her, too? No, Mom was just playing the role of the grown-up. Respect the benefactor's wishes, no questions asked.

Maybe Dr. Hsu was right. Maybe Devon was starting to get paranoid. But, could anxiety be considered paranoia if there were really good reasons for it? Or is that what paranoid people told themselves to justify further paranoia?

Now "we're" in a downward spiral of paranoia, Devon thought with a groan.

Lying in bed wasn't going to help her get more answers. It was Sunday morning, and she had someone she needed to talk to.

CLEO'S ROOM WAS EMPTY, along with over half the other rooms in Morgan House. The black Calvin Klein bedspread was tucked in without a wrinkle. Cleo's makeup was gone from her dresser, too. She must be out of town for the weekend. But she'd have to be back at some point today.

Devon caught a glimpse of herself in the mirror on Cleo's closet door. Her hair was spilling in all directions from her ponytail, and she had a pillow crease denting her left cheek. Yet it was just last night Bodhi had his fingers threaded through her hair while they kissed. Devon needed to see Cleo before she could think about Bodhi anymore. Was she to blame for Bodhi and Cleo breaking up?

No, that was impossible. Besides, both of them had told her the same thing in different ways, reiterating what she already knew: they were very different people, fashion vs. ocean, airbrush tan vs. year-round natural tan. It didn't seem like Cleo was especially heartbroken over Bodhi. She was the one who'd gone off in search of Eli, their mysterious dimpled waiter.

So why did kissing Bodhi feel like a betrayal?

It didn't matter. Cleo probably understood Devon better than anyone on campus, better even than Presley. Besides, Devon couldn't wait to tell Cleo the dirt that she had on Eli, thanks to the Elliot siblings. Though, knowing Cleo, the fact that Eli was a hired evildoer might even make her like him more.

Devon scribbled on a Post-it pad on Cleo's desk.

Miss me? Find me when you're back. –D.

With that, Devon hurried from Morgan House and walked to the edge of the hillside. Her eyes traced the sloping green lawn that met with thick bushes, giving way to pine trees and redwoods, the wilderness below. Dark gray clouds rolled in from the ocean. Cotton-like wisps of cloud crept through Reed's grapevines.

She wondered if Bodhi was working in the guesthouse.

What was going to happen with her and Bodhi now? Had he thought that kiss through? What if she'd said no or pulled away? Would it have ruined their friendship? Too many hypotheticals to consider . . . She needed something to distract her busy brain. And she knew exactly what that distraction needed to be. The kiss had made her forget a very important piece of business—namely, that she still hadn't opened Reed's diary.

DEVON'S BACKPACK WAS STILL on the floor where she had left it last night.

She frowned as she picked it up, thinking of how red her face must have been when she'd dashed into the dorm thirty seconds before the curfew bell rang. Ms. Hadden had frowned out the door while it swung closed, as if expecting to see a boy running back to his dorm with a blanket over her shoulder. But no, there was no boy. None that she could see, anyway.

Devon Mackintosh, on time. Check.

Next time, Devon wouldn't wait until 9:50 to dash. She flopped on her bed and pulled out the diary, careful to avoid creasing the brittle paper.

Jan. 1, 1942

Dr. Keaton has changed my life a second time. First when he accepted me into his physics program at Berkeley. Now he has invited Athena and me to stay and work with him on a top-secret new project for the war effort. I'm probably not even supposed to say the words "top secret," but it is a secret, even from us. Dr. Keaton doesn't even really know the true nature of our work, but he believes that is for our safety, which I'm happy to believe.

It's hard to describe our new home. Near Santa Cruz and up the hillside some. An Army jeep manned by a Corporal Grayson drove Athena and me over from Berkeley. Dr. Keaton's lab wasn't much more than a tent with wooden planks for floors and metal tables stacked with boxes.

"We're getting the buildings put up in the next month or so. Would hate to have our work affected by the elements, you see."

Those were his exact words, the words I remember most clearly. The rest is a fog of excitement. He asked Athena and me to quit Berkley and live up here and work with him. I am so honored. It is the noblest opportunity.

And he did share <u>one</u> secret.

He introduced us to someone, a woman, when he invited us for tea in another tent. She wore tan riding pants and was putting cups and a teapot on a tray. I could hear a faint whistle from the metal kettle on the stove.

"Hana, we have guests," Dr. Keaton said to her.

Instantly we realized she was Japanese. She had a milky complexion, more fair-skinned than the Chinese workers I was used to seeing around Oakland. He knew that Athena and I would be shocked, and he wanted to gauge our reaction. And it's not like we have anything against a Japanese person. It's just that since the bombing of Pearl Harbor last month, the whole country is looking at Japanese people differently.

Hana led us to a nearby picnic table, where she poured tea for each of us. Dr. Keaton watched us the whole time. It wasn't until then that we put it together that Hana was Keaton's wife. Both of them wear simple gold wedding bands. Keaton kept a tender hand on her back while she poured.

Once we were all served, Keaton asked if he could speak with me privately. I assumed he was going to discuss more logistics with moving Athena and me up to the hill, but no. He told me that he and Hana have been married for three years. She was born and raised in Oakland, but he feels like the anti-Japanese sentiment will only get worse in the city. He doesn't need to convince me. I know how bad it is, but listening to him was tough. Last week the grocery store owner down the street from them wouldn't even sell groceries to Hana until Keaton came and intervened.

The Army has done a background check on Hana, and she was cleared to be here with Keaton, but he is not allowed to discuss his work with her. That's why he wants to make sure Athena would come to the hill with me. Hana needs another woman around to talk to, a friend. They plan on making a permanent home on the hillside. But he needs to know we're okay with Hana. What could I say? Of course we are.

By the end of the conversation, Keaton had agreed to build a house for Athena and me, hired me at $25 a week, and confirmed that we would start by the end of the month. And I still don't know what we'll be doing.

Devon drifted off to sleep. She dreamt about Hutch. She saw his wild hair and clever smile as they walked around the empty hillside. He reached out for her hand, but the wind pulled her away from him. She tried calling, but the wind seemed to absorb her voice, and then she was falling and falling down the cliff side until she landed on the hard cement of the Palace. Eric was standing over her with the spyglass in his hands. He used it to take a swing at her—

Devon jerked up in bed.

The bright morning had turned into a gray afternoon.

She took a few deep breaths, shaking off the nightmare, then eyed the diary beside her. It was difficult to imagine a time when this hillside wasn't dotted with dorms, dining halls, gyms, a pool. It must have been amazing to be up here before the school was built. So Reed had a wife, Athena. She'd never even considered who Hutch's grandmother was. She'd never really considered The Keaton School as a product of the actual Dr. Keaton, the person—someone who'd led an entirely different life before the school existed. And if Dr. Keaton had a wife, why was there no mention of her anywhere on campus?

CHAPTER 7

Sunday dinners were a generally depressing affair. Devon knew that the stories and the buzz from weekends off campus would fall silent upon arrival in the dining hall. She sighed as she gathered her dinner on a plastic tray. At least tonight was cheeseburger night. Fries, salad, and even a berry cobbler concoction would suffice to dull the buildup of yet another week at Keaton. She approached Dr. Mettier at the check-in table. Another day, another "Devon Mackintosh, check."

When someone slapped Devon's butt, she nearly dropped her tray on Dr. Mettier's lap.

Cleo was standing behind Devon in her uniform of motorcycle boots, black leggings, and a black leather jacket with zippers going in every direction. She pulled the black knitted hat off her head and shook out her chin-length hair. "How did you survive without me this weekend, Mackintosh?" Cleo waved at Dr. Mettier as he checked her off his list with a satisfied grunt.

Devon's smile faltered. A wave of guilt washed over her. But . . . why *did* she feel guilty about Bodhi? He and Cleo were over. He'd made the move. They'd shared a kiss; that was it. "Wanna eat with me?" she finally managed.

Cleo sneered at the lopsided cheeseburger and wilted lettuce they were supposed to call dinner on Devon's tray. "You okay? The food is supposed to make you sick *after* you eat it, remember?"

"Funny," Devon said, regaining some composure. "So?"

"Hell, no. I made a point to eat before I got back. How about I just keep you company while you eat?"

Devon made a beeline toward a table in a corner in the back of the dining hall. Although the dinner rush seemed to have died out, a corner table away from eavesdropping ears was still a minor coup.

"Is this about snooping around my room?" Cleo asked, a twinkle in her eye. "I saw your note when I got back. Come on, *dis-moi*, how much did you enjoy going through my stuff?"

Devon took a bite of her burger. It tasted like foamy filler. Maybe the whole thing wasn't as big a deal as she thought. "I didn't see anything that belongs to me, let's just say that."

Cleo sat back in her chair and crossed her arms. "So? What's the deal? Is this business or social? With you, I never know."

Devon put her food down. "I just wanted to check with you. About you and Bodhi."

"He kissed you, didn't he?" Cleo asked point-blank.

Devon's face flushed.

"He did, he did, he did!" Cleo slapped her palms on their table, taunting Devon with a wicked, delighted laugh.

"I really wasn't expecting it, I swear," Devon gasped, relief flooding through her. "But it happened, and I guess I was, I mean, I am happy it did. So it's okay with you? Please say it's okay with you." She took another bite of her hamburger, just to give herself something to do.

Cleo smiled. "You're sweet, Dev. Bodhi and me . . . it was just a few hookups, and I felt as guilty as you do now, if you want to know the truth. I always knew something was lurking there between you two. Of course you should go for it." She shook salt over Devon's French fries before picking at a few. "And trust me, Bodhi never does anything he doesn't want to do. He and Raven have been calling their own shots for a while now. If he kissed you, it wasn't an accident. The guy likes you. My advice? Try to enjoy it. You do know how to enjoy things, yes?"

Devon managed another smirk and dropped her hamburger, resisting the temptation to reach across the table and hug Cleo. "Okay, so here's the other thing. Remember your waiter crush on New Year's? Dimples? Eli, or that's at least what he told me his name was?"

Cleo nodded, intrigued now.

She and Bodhi really *were* just a hookup, Devon realized. "Get this—he was using someone else's ID that night."

"Wait, are you saying my crush was your attacker?" Cleo leaned back. Her boot tapped the wooden floor. "Just my luck. Why do I always fall for the dark and disturbed ones?"

Devon blinked. Did Cleo think she was joking?

Cleo's face fell. "Oh, Dev, I'm sorry." She leaned over the table. "I'm totally not belittling your attack. But you get it, right? We have got to find normal, non-betraying boyfriends. And it sounds like you have . . ." Cleo dropped off in mid-sentence. Her snarky grin returned, and she tilted her head at the table behind them.

Devon twisted around to see Grant sitting down.

He caught their eyes. Devon quickly looked away. What she wouldn't give to forget that whole Grant debacle of last semester. Her cheeks burned redder than they had last night at check-in, remembering how much she had trusted him. *Lying jerk*, she thought for the hundredth time. Luckily Grant had stayed clear of her this semester. She secretly hoped he was too ashamed to come near. Living with that kind of shame only seemed fair.

"So I'm going to go into the city next weekend," Devon whispered, back squarely turned on Grant. "Try to find this Eli guy. You want in?"

Cleo finished Devon's French fries. "Don't know. Bodhi going to be there?"

"Yeah, probably. Is that weird?"

"How about this? My mom's got some spa thing in Switzerland the rest of the month. Why don't we get signed out next weekend to my parents' penthouse near the marina? We have a fun getaway weekend, and if the Dreadlocked Duo want to make an appearance and find our waiter, then we're *all* in?"

Devon had to laugh. "The Dreadlocked Duo. They are gonna hate that."

Cleo shrugged. "Haters gonna hate. What can you do?" She brought her head closer to Devon's and jutted her chin out in Grant's direction. "Wait a sec. Who's the fresh blood sitting with Grant?"

Devon turned to see a perfect stranger plunking his tray down by Grant. Needless to say, a perfect stranger appearing mid-year at Keaton was newsworthy, especially someone who looked like *this*. Blond hair in an almost buzz cut, dark eyebrows, and deep brown eyes. Devon couldn't help but stare. Neither could Cleo, of course. Grant leaned over and whispered something. Fresh Blood looked up from his burger and saluted Devon and Cleo.

"Ladies," he said in a loud, confident voice with an accent Devon couldn't place. "Good evening."

Devon whipped around to face Cleo, whose cheeks were pink.

"They must have pulled someone off the waitlist mid-year," Cleo muttered, smiling in spite of herself. "Man, someone's parents must have wanted him to get a Keaton education. Starting mid-year has to seriously suck." She started typing something into her phone.

"What are you doing?" Devon asked.

"Texting a friend at St. Matthews in the city. Wait-listers usually come locally. The international kids have too many visa hoops to jump through to make last-minute decisions. We gotta get the intel on our newbie because you know how it goes; girls are gonna be all over that like the summer sale at Barney's."

Devon sneaked another peek in his direction, and Fresh Blood smiled back, clearly enjoying the attention. This time she noticed something else: two perfect dimples, one on each cheek. He was almost *too* perfect looking. Her heart clenched for a moment as she turned back to her food, her appetite gone. Had this guy had taken the spot that had been freed by Hutch's death?

"Unbelievable," Cleo said, as if cursing the people who created him. She went back to her phone, fingers moving faster than before. "This is total trouble. Dev, you know better than anyone, I'm a sucker for a guy with dimples. Way more than dreads."

CHAPTER 8

Devon still had a few homework questions to finish before first-period chemistry, so she made sure to get to the classroom early to work in silence, far away from the bustle of her dorm. Just her luck—the chem lab doors were locked. She made due sitting in the deserted hallway. Usually Mr. Denny was in his classroom at this hour, slugging coffee from a thermos and prepping for that day's lesson. So apparently even guys like Mr. Denny had a hard time moving first thing Monday morning. It was reassuring somehow. Teachers and faculty members were human beings, too, after all—including geniuses, Dr. Hsu among them.

The linoleum floor felt cold on the back of Devon's legs, even through her jeans. She opened her laptop and tried to concentrate. The door at the end of the hall opened with a *clang*, and Scott Jacoby appeared in his usual Keaton pajama pants and oversized backpack. A day student with nothing else going on outside of Keaton, he'd no doubt answered the questions by Friday afternoon and done the extra credit work, too. He threw off the grading curve in most of his classes. On the other hand, maybe if she flirted just a little bit, he might be inclined to let her copy the final few answers from his work. She stood up to greet Scott when a classroom door opened down the hall.

Devon froze. It was C.C. Tran, dressed in a white pencil skirt with matching blazer and clutching a Starbucks cup. She exited the room with Mr. Denny. She had a few books tucked under her arm. Devon recognized the blue cover of her own current chemistry textbook. *Maya's mom is collecting homework. That means Maya is still enrolled.* They may have given up Maya's room, but presumably she was trying to keep up with the school year. Maya was somewhere doing her homework. Before Devon could fully formulate her thoughts, she'd hurried past Scott and planted herself right in front of Maya's mother.

C.C. looked at Devon expectantly as if she were an assistant interrupting a meeting with C.C.'s board of directors.

"Hi, Ms. Tran? You don't know me, but I'm a friend of Maya's. Devon Mackintosh. I just wanted to see if Maya is okay. Does she need anything?"

C.C. pulled her thin lips into a tight smile. She looked over Devon's head at Mr. Denny as if to say, *These kids just don't stop, do they?*

Mr. Denny took the woman's hand in an empathetic shake. "Thanks for coming by, Ms. Tran. I'm sure we'll talk soon."

C.C. withdrew with the same tight smile and waited until Mr. Denny was opening his classroom door down the hall before turning back to Devon. "Devon, you said?" she asked brusquely. "Maya is doing fine. I'm collecting some work for her so she doesn't fall too far behind the rest of her year."

"Is she coming back to Keaton?"

"Not sure. We're still discussing next year. There are many options to consider . . ." C.C. started scrolling through her emails on her gold-plated phone. The silent way of saying, *Get the hell out of my face, kid.*

Devon held her ground. "I'd love to talk with her. Maybe you'll tell her to give me a ring? Or email or something?"

C.C. looked up from her phone. "Maya's not taking calls right now. But when she does, I'll tell her you asked after her. Okay?"

Before Devon could respond, the woman sashayed down the hall. Devon had no idea what C.C. could possibly mean. *Not taking calls?* Had her parents placed Maya under their own version of house arrest? It seemed that way. Since she'd left school, Devon had tried to find her online, but her Instagram and Twitter accounts had become inactive.

But one thing was certain: Maya had not fallen off the face of the earth entirely. She'd be nearly six months pregnant at this point. Devon had a hard time imagining Maya's small frame with a baby belly. Had Maya purposefully withdrawn from public, or had her parents forced seclusion upon her?

As the first-period bell rang, Devon allowed herself the thought at the root of it all, the one that was nagging at her deep down. If she could find out what was going on with Maya, then she could share that information with Eric. And maybe then Eric would be more inclined to answer *her* questions.

SECOND PERIOD WAS EVEN worse than chemistry; it was her next session with Dr. Hsu.

Devon found a seat on a bench next to the science building. She tried to wrap her head around the idea that in three minutes, she would be expected to pour out her deepest, darkest secrets to a woman who wanted to prove Devon was crazy.

On the other hand, it had been helpful. Last session Devon had even enjoyed letting Dr. Hsu believe that Devon's stories were simply paranoia getting out of control. A part of her was curious just how far she could milk that angle. After all, everyone had thought she was crazy for believing that Hutch hadn't killed himself.

But honestly, if the school administration were sidelining her as unreliable and delusional, then they wouldn't plan on reinstating the peer counselor program anytime soon. Which was fine. Devon didn't need that distraction right now. Last semester Keaton had lost three students—four if you included Hutch. But the other three were in the program. Between Isla's parents sending her to rehab, Matt's choosing to leave school for an indefinite "surfing hiatus" (his words), and Maya's pregnancy, Devon's record of helping students cope wasn't exactly stellar.

Another thought crept into her mind. The powers-that-be at Keaton weren't trying to pin any of that on *her*, were they?

She had always assumed that implicating a student in negligent peer counseling—the pilot program, no less—would also make the school look bad. But maybe she had Keaton's puppet masters wrong. Maybe the school was looking for a way to take her down with the other students. One less troublemaker?

No, there was no way they would do that.

Besides, it wasn't just pure morbid curiosity that made Devon want to play into their fears and be the head case Dr. Hsu was hoping she would be. She wanted to buy some time for herself, to keep them interested in and aware of her fears. If someone had tried to murder her on New Year's Eve, that kind of publicity wouldn't look good for Keaton, either. They would keep her safe, if only to salvage their reputation in the wake of the Hutchins scandal. Especially if the Hutchins family *was* her benefactor . . .

I'm not a pawn, she thought.

But in thinking that, didn't she simply prove Dr. Hsu's theory that she *was* paranoid?

∞

Session #2: Devon Mackintosh
Monday, January 14, 2013

"So." Dr. Hsu flashed her professional detached smile and tucked her lap blanket under her knees. "Have you been keeping up with your schoolwork this semester? Second-semester juniors can often get overwhelmed by their commitments this time of year."

"I think it's been okay. Just trying to handle what comes." Devon made a point of studying her fingernails.

"Have you been giving any thought to college? A college trip during spring break? That's generally considered one of the most advantageous times to go."

Devon shrugged. "Presley and I were thinking of going to the East Coast. Which schools out there do you think would suit me best?"

Dr. Hsu laughed. "I'm sure the college advisory office is probably a better place to discuss this. What about the other things? Have you given any more thought to what we discussed last session?"

Game on again, Devon thought. "Well, I haven't found my attacker yet, if that's what you're asking."

"We both know that's not what I was asking." Dr. Hsu kept her eyes focused on Devon's own. "We're here to discuss the connections you've been drawing between traumatic incidents in your life. Nobody is underestimating your trauma."

Now it was Devon's turn to laugh. "Jeez, that's nice," she said sarcastically. "Anyway, isn't that what those bumper stickers say? *We're all connected?*"

"Devon, I'm serious," Dr. Hsu said gently. "But between the trauma of what happened on the yacht and what happened to Jason Hutchins . . . that's a lot to handle for anyone. Do you still see those events as being connected?"

So she really does want me to believe that I'm paranoid, Devon thought, surprised at her own anger. *And she clearly doesn't have much interest in actually doing the work of counseling me, because I left the door wide open for that kind of reassurance. If I were sitting in that chair, I wouldn't have said, "Devon, I'm serious"; I would have said, "Devon, I'm here to help you." But fine. Let the fun begin . . .*

"Yes, I do. I totally think they're connected. And you know what else? There's a guy that works in the kitchen. Ricky, I think his name is. He's been weird. Smiling at me like he knows my secret. I think he knows who's behind what happened to me on New Year's Eve."

Dr. Hsu broke eye contact to write something in her notebook.

And just to push the envelope, Devon added, "I think the entire kitchen staff knows what happened."

Nothing. No response. "How have you been sleeping?" Dr. Hsu asked, as if the question was somehow related to the nonsense Devon had just spewed. Maybe a Stanford PhD wasn't worth all that much, after all. Or maybe hers was phony.

"Terribly," Devon answered. "I just don't feel safe anymore." *Would telling her that I'm hearing voices be too much?*

Dr. Hsu put down her notebook and reached for the drawer in the small end table next to her chair. She pulled out a palm-sized pad.

Prescriptions.

Bingo, Devon thought, clenching her jaw. *Now the real motives are coming out.* The Keaton School wanted to medicate her. Of course. This was not paranoia. This was reality. No doubt they wanted to lull her into some zombie-like state so she'd shut her mouth and stop poking around places where she wasn't welcome— be it Cleo's yacht or the school's alumni scholarship fund.

Dr. Hsu scribbled something on the pad and tore it off the top.

"This is a prescription for Vericyl," she said, the detached smile back in place. "You'll need to give this to Nurse Reilly to have it filled. It's a newer drug, but it's been proven to be very effective for post-traumatic stress in teenagers."

Devon took the paper and studied Dr. Hsu's precise cursive script.

"I can understand if you're conflicted about this diagnosis," Dr. Hsu said. "But Devon, it's nothing to be ashamed of. You've suffered, and you have to come to terms with that. Add to the mix that this is an anxious time in your life in general."

"I'm . . ." Devon took a deep breath. "I just want to get back to my old self." For the first time today, she had told Dr. Hsu the truth.

Dr. Hsu nodded. "I'm so happy you said that. I think we should start with this dose and keep close contact. For our next session, I'd like to see you come up with a college-trip plan, one we can discuss. Is that something you think you can do?"

"Yes, Dr. Hsu. Definitely. Next week then. Thanks."

Devon got up slowly, just to make sure she wasn't misreading the situation. Was Dr. Hsu on her side, after all? When she also stood up, Devon knew she was allowed to leave, too. *Wow, that was easy,* she thought. *Maybe too easy.*

"One more thing. Are there any side effects to the medication?" she asked.

"Nothing to be frightened of," Dr. Hsu said. "Nurse Reilly will discuss all of that with you. And of course you'll need to discuss this prescription with your mother before you fill it. I'd encourage her to call me. I won't discuss any specifics of what goes on here with her; that's between us and us alone. But she needs to be on the same page in terms of medication."

Nothing to be frightened of, Devon repeated silently. Nope, just that Dr. Hsu believed that Devon *was* paranoid and delusional. But that was what Devon wanted, right? She wanted Keaton to be aware of her, watching out for her physical safety, while she continued the search for her attacker. In another way, it made her more paranoid than ever that she was playing into Keaton's hands in their desire to forget about the Hutch ugliness, to wipe it clean, and to move forward.

"Don't worry," Devon finally said. "My mom will get it. She's a nurse."

RAVEN WAS SITTING ON the bench outside Dr. Hsu's office, her cheeks blotchy and swollen. She hugged her knees against her chest, rocking back and forth, her dreadlocks in disarray. She looked up when Devon opened the door.

"Raven . . . ?" Devon started.

"Reed's dead."

Raven jumped up and buried her head against Devon's outstretched arm. Her body shook with sobs. Devon stood still, unable to move, unable to do anything but hold Raven and let her cry. She'd known this was coming, but she couldn't accept that it would be so soon.

Across the mountainside, she could see Reed's grapevines and the rooftop of his house. *He's really gone.* It didn't seem to jibe with the beautiful vista. Even so close to death, he'd been so alive.

Behind them, the door opened, and Dr. Hsu appeared, a bag slung over her shoulder. She looked over at Devon and noticed the crying girl on her arm. She stiffened, and her brow furrowed, but then she gave Devon the slightest smile before lowering her eyes and walking in the other direction. Of course: she wanted to be compassionate, but she wasn't allowed to acknowledge their relationship outside of their session. Devon could relate. She almost felt sorry for the woman. At least she had some more evidence that Dr. Hsu was, indeed, a human being. Five minutes ago, she hadn't been so sure.

Raven wiped her cheeks with the back of her sleeve. "I can't be here right now," she breathed. "I'm sorry, I just . . ."

"Don't apologize. Come on, I'll walk you to your car." Devon had US history next period, but Mr. Blakely would understand if she was a few minutes late.

Raven's red Volvo was parked in the corner of the lot. There was a bright pink splotch on the hood of the car. As they drew closer, Devon realized it was a cluster of pink flowers: two roses and a few wildflowers. They looked like someone had torn them from one of the gardens near the teachers' homes on the edge of the hill.

A piece of paper was wrapped around the ragged stems.

Devon looked at Raven, but she only shook her head. With shaky fingers, Devon unwrapped the paper. Written in pencil were the words, I'm sorry for your loss. The letters were narrow and crooked, as if whoever had left it had written the note quickly. Devon looked up at Raven, whose tears had momentarily stopped.

"Who else knows about Reed?" Devon asked.

Raven shook her head again. "Bodhi just texted me during the last class. I didn't see it until I got out." She sniffed the flowers. Her eyes started watering again as Devon handed her the note. "I have to go. Bodhi'll need me." She frowned at the crumpled piece of paper. "You think this is bad?"

"I don't know. Maybe you have an admirer?" Devon offered.

"With a scary knack for gathering information?"

Devon bit her lip. Paranoia or not, it's what she had been thinking, too.

CHAPTER 9

March 30, 1942

I've been so busy! No time to write. There is so much going on. I got married! Dr. Keaton married us on the hillside on March 1st, my birthday. Athena's parents weren't able to travel from Washington, but they sent a lovely box with rose petals for us to scatter along our small wedding aisle. We exchanged rings at sunset. It will forever be the happiest day of my life. I want this project to be a success just to keep that smile on Athena's face as long as possible.

Athena and Hana have been working together, building a vegetable garden, getting a kitchen cabin up and running. Athena even planted a few grapevines. Her father used to make homemade wine, apparently. As always, Athena continues to surprise me with her talents. And now that we're more confident that I won't have to ship out for the war, we're going to try to have children.

We feel guilty being so happy up here. This hillside has allowed us to live different lives than the people in the cities. Just last week we heard from General Grayson about the mandatory Japanese evacuations. Notices posted all over San Francisco, Berkeley, and Oakland telling Japanese families to pack up their houses, belongings, leave pets behind, and take only what they could carry.

Athena says that Hana doesn't discuss it with her, but we can only imagine what that must feel like. Isn't this exactly what we are fighting against in Europe? I know Dr. Keaton is trying to keep Hana away from the bad news. He also seems to keep her away from our work in the lab. I understand. It's for her own protection. I hope the Army doesn't change its mind about giving Hana security clearance.

Work continues here with Dr. Keaton, the fast-neutron research that we began at the Berkeley labs with Oppie. And just yesterday we had a new arrival to our small hillside community, Edward Dover. He used to be a research-and-development biologist at Merck Pharmaceuticals.

Edward's a funny guy. He's short and round and never stops moving or talking. I didn't know that much about the pharmaceutical companies until now. Edward is full of ideas. He explained how we could sell a patent to Merck and live off the royalties for the rest of our lives. He is certain that what we're doing up here on the hill will bring about a handful of new patents when the war is over.

"It's closer than you think," he keeps saying. It's like there's a small motor inside of him that won't quit. Edward says that the Army brought him into our project to help coordinate Dr. Keaton's progress with other teams around the country.

For some reason—and I write this only because Athena has noticed it, too—it doesn't seem like Edward has Dr. Keaton's full trust yet. Probably thinks he's reporting back to the Army. Maybe he is, but if I can work with him to set up a patent like he says, it would mean everything for my family's future. I have to think that way now.

THE SERVICE WAS SMALLER than Devon would have expected. Reed had apparently written out detailed instructions for his funeral, not that she was surprised. He even hired a local party planner just to make sure Raven and Bodhi didn't get stuck with the brunt of the work. Of course Bill and Mitzi showed up, Mitzi shaking her head in a constant state of disagreeing with Reed's decisions. Bill, in a black suit that Devon recognized from Hutch's funeral, smiled in silence. Here at least, he seemed to be playing the role of dutiful son.

Devon stood in the corner of Reed's living room, taking in the scene while sipping a glass of sparkling water. The bartender silently poured drinks for the somber guests. He was about Eli's age (no dimples) and Devon wondered if he worked for the same catering company that Cleo's father had used on New Year's Eve.

Bill began to work the room, shaking hands with a bunch of men in black suits Devon had never seen before. No doubt they were here for Bill, not Reed. Cleo, also at home in another all-black ensemble, crossed the room toward Devon with drinks in hand, raising an eyebrow along the way.

"Got the bartender to slip a little vodka in here. Take a sip." Cleo held her glass out to Devon.

"I'm cool," Devon replied, still canvassing the crowd.

Cleo followed Devon's gaze around the room. "The suits? Probably the TerraTech board of directors. They've all come just to kiss Bill's ass, is my guess."   "Why wasn't Reed a part of TerraTech?" Devon asked. "He was a scientist, too."

"Who knows?" Cleo took a big swig of her drink. "All Bodhi could ever figure out was that Reed didn't agree with the work Bill was doing. Don't know why though. TerraTech is, like, some major Fortune 500 company. Not Reed's style. But clearly that family knows how to make money."

Devon caught a glimpse of Bodhi and Raven slipping into the living room through a side door. Both had their dreads pulled back in neat ponytails. Raven wore an elegant black dress; Bodhi's dark suit was indistinguishable from the cluster around Bill. It looked brand new, neatly pressed, a perfect fit. Devon thought of their faded black outfits at Hutch's funeral only months ago. Then they were friendly misfits, whereas now they gracefully blended in among the high-class crowd. Devon stared down at her feet, suddenly feeling claustrophobic.

She hadn't had a chance to talk with Bodhi since their kiss. He'd flashed her a brief, sad smile over Reed's coffin during the service. Did that count as flirting? No. Of course not. What was she thinking? In fact, Devon realized, *flirting* and *coffin* were words that shouldn't be used in the same sentence ever again.

Cleo handed her drink to Raven. Bodhi sidled up to Devon but avoided her eyes. "Don't worry. It's vodka," Cleo said.

Raven took the glass and drained it. After a small shake of her head and a vodka-soaked exhale, she spoke. Her eyes started watering. "We just met with Reed's lawyer about his will." She shook her head again and looked to Bodhi.

"He left us everything," Bodhi stated.

Devon blinked several times. Even Cleo was speechless.

"Everything?" Devon finally repeated.

She scanned the massive living room. This whole house, the guest house, the vineyard . . .

"Everything," Raven said, as if she could see Devon's mental checklist. "Except the land. He donated that to Keaton, for the school legacy or something."

"He put his patents in a trust in our names. The future of his work is in our hands." Bodhi spoke as if he was reciting what the lawyer had just said to him. His tone was empty, as if none of it were real.

"*Elliot.*"

The voice was a growl. Bill Hutchins broke from his huddle and made his way across the living room in three long strides. Devon took a step back. Raven's shoulders hunched up, and she leaned against Bodhi, who stretched an arm in front of her. "You put him up to this, didn't you?" Bill spat. "What did you do, give him drugs?"

"Mr. Hutchins, we didn't know that this was Reed's plan," Bodhi said in a calm, measured voice. "He never told us, and we would have never asked. But we also want to respect his wishes." It was hard not to be impressed that in front of the towering six-foot-plus Bill Hutchins, Bodhi stood straight. He didn't even bristle.

"Cute." Bill's eyes narrowed. His lips twisted in an angry smirk. "Respect his wishes all you want, but my lawyers are going to go to town on you two. The future of this family will not be determined by a pair of surf bums from Monte Vista." Bill glared at Bodhi just long enough to make Devon more uncomfortable than she already was. She couldn't breathe again until Bill had whirled and stomped toward the side door.

The crowd around her began to whisper.

Through the open door, Devon spotted an old man with a wooden cane in the garden, flanked by a man about Bill's age. Both were short, round, with the same pug noses—a father-and-son pair, no doubt. They looked familiar, but Devon couldn't place them. Probably another Keaton family. The old man waved Bill over.

After a quick, hushed conversation, Bill shook hands with each of them. Devon realized she was staring. She turned away, but caught a glimpse of C.C. Tran.

Who had Maya in tow.

Devon's eyes widened. *Right*, she realized. Those two guys were Edward Dover and his son, Edward Junior, Maya's dad. Behind her father, Maya kept her eyes glued to the floor. Devon couldn't blame her. Under the flowing black dress, Maya's pregnant belly was getting too big to ignore.

She and Bodhi traded looks. Did Eric know that Maya was here? It was doubtful, unless Eric had found some way to communicate with her. After the service, two security guards had escorted him back to a private town car and presumably driven him back to San Francisco. Devon had so many questions. But Maya stayed in the shadows, hidden behind her father. There had to be a way to get her alone.

Cleo nudged Devon. "We have to say something to her."

"It doesn't look like she can get away from her parents."

"Shall we sorority-girl her?"

Devon had no idea what it meant to *sorority-girl* someone, but she did know that the world of this funeral—with its wealth, its privilege, and its reputations to protect—was Cleo's, not hers. She nodded. Before Devon could protest, Cleo grabbed her wrist and led the way.

"Maiii-ya!" Cleo squealed.

Devon winced. The decibel levels were way too high and inappropriate. But now she understood Cleo's strategy. Everyone would stare for a second, then turn away. Their embarrassment would guarantee the three girls a few precious moments of privacy.

"Ohmygodddd!!" Devon tried to get her voice as high as Cleo's.

Maya's face fell as they burst outside and swept her into a hug. She looked as if she wanted to melt into the garden flagstones. Overflowing with excitement, Devon and Cleo pushed her past the Dover men and C.C. Tran.

"What the hell are you guys doing?" Maya hissed.

Devon glanced over her shoulder as Cleo fawned over Maya's long hair and pregnant belly. Sure enough, everyone was making a concerted effort not to look in their direction—in particular, Maya's own family.

"Dude, where the hell have you been?" Cleo whispered in a normal voice.

"Eric was trying to find you," Devon added. "What's going on? Are your parents locking you away in some attic somewhere?"

Maya glanced past them nervously. She swallowed and backed toward a hedge at the edge of the patio, making sure to stay safely shielded behind Devon and Cleo. "They're going to send me away to have the baby," she whispered. "One of those homes for pregnant girls. St. Mary's. It's in Montana."

Devon couldn't believe what she was hearing. Were the Dovers really that unsympathetic? Didn't they have any compassion at all? It sounded like something out of some bad Dickensian novel, not the way any normal family would deal with a teen pregnancy in the 21st century. "What about Eric? Are they pressing charges?"

Maya bit her lip. "They're going to stay out of Eric's trial. Leave that to the Hutchins family. They think the baby will . . ." Maya trailed off as she rubbed her hands up and down her belly. "They think the baby will help heal things. Get rid of the bad blood between the families. Bring us closer."

Cleo hiccupped and frowned. "You mean, the Dovers *want* to

get in bed with the Hutchinses? I thought you all hated each other. I mean, minus you and Eric. But the rest of you. And if they're sending you to Montana, how is that going to help?"

Devon cringed slightly. Cleo probably shouldn't go for a refill.

Maya shrugged. "Honestly? I think they just want me in a safe place until the baby arrives. Away from distractions and worry. Away from Eric, too. I mean, I can't imagine what my parents feel about Eric, especially now, after Hutch . . ." She caught Devon's gaze, then turned back to the lump under her dress. "But the fact remains that this baby carries both families' blood. My dad thought—"

"Maya, we're leaving," C.C. Tran interrupted.

Devon had no idea how long Maya's mom had been standing right behind her. It didn't matter; the message was clear. Maya was not to associate with her old friends anymore.

Maya ducked her head. "Sorry, guys. I gotta go." She squeezed Devon's hand. C.C. shot a disapproving glare at both Cleo and Devon before sinking her manicured nails into Maya's upper arm and whisking her quickly from the garden. Maya almost tripped as she struggled to keep up. After another quick handshake with Bill Hutchins, the Dover men hurried after them, vanishing back into the house.

"What do you think is really going on?" Cleo whispered to Devon. "This can't be about kissing and making up, can it?"

The answer hadn't even occurred to Devon until she saw those final handshakes. There was no warmth in the gestures. No offering of condolences for a bereaved son over the loss of his father, no hint of gratitude for a baby on the way, nothing *personal*. They were the cold handshakes of a deal.

"This is about business," she murmured, almost to herself.

"What do you mean?" Cleo asked.

"What's Maya's dad's company do again?"

"Dover Industries. Pharmaceuticals. Like, in a big way," Cleo said. She grinned and hiccupped again. "Why do I get the feeling like calling my stockbroker would be a good idea?"

"This isn't about uniting the two families," Devon said. "It's about uniting TerraTech and Dover Industries. Because there's no way that would have ever happened while Reed was alive."

CHAPTER 10

In the days following Reed's funeral, Maya didn't respond to any of Devon's texts or emails. Devon had been expecting radio silence, obviously. And she had to hand it to the Dovers: instead of slinking away in disgrace, they were figuring out a way to use the unborn Hutchins-Dover child as a white flag between the families. Or were they figuring out a way to use Maya as a Trojan horse? Would the baby somehow destroy the Hutchins family and secure the Dovers' power over some business merger?

Did it even matter?

Devon lay in her bed, relishing the last cozy moments under her comforter before classes that morning. She wished that she could somehow fill the queasy pit in her stomach with that same warmth. What Bodhi was up to, surfing? At his computer? Thinking about her? Thinking about the fact that he was now a multimillionaire?

They hadn't spoken since the funeral. Of course they hadn't. Bodhi had always loved Reed like a grandfather, and now Bodhi had proof that Reed felt the same way about him. But that kiss . . .

Maybe he'd just been seeking solace where he could find it. Like he kept saying, Devon's problems were a welcome distraction, a lot more pleasant than worrying about Reed. Maybe it had been a one-time thing. Maybe he'd changed his mind. Her thoughts returned to the training Mr. Robins had given her last year: *If a subject obsesses about what they can't control, gently remind them of what they can control, and emphasize its importance.*

Right. She couldn't control Bodhi's feelings any more than she could control the rain that had landed for the winter, or the frigid wind that came with it. If he wanted to get in touch, he would. Same with Maya.

THE NEXT WEEK WAS a blur of Keaton routine: falling asleep mid-homework, waking up to the patter of rain, pulling on her mud-encrusted boots. She'd run through the rain to class, run to the dining hall for meals, and run back to her room to deal with yet another avalanche of assignments. At least she *could* control her GPA.

Wednesday night, Mrs. Hadden pounded on her door. "Eleven P.M.! Lights out!"

Devon jumped. She realized her yellow highlighter had been hovering over the same page in her US history textbook for the last twenty minutes. Okay, she was done. Unfurled herself from pretzel position on her bed, she shook out the pins and needles running up her calf. *Ugh.* She slipped out of her jeans and threw them onto her closet shelf.

A slip of white paper peeking from one of the back pockets caught her eye. She plucked it from the pocket. Dr. Hsu's prescription for Vericyl. Devon still hadn't mentioned it to her mom; she hadn't even had a real conversation beyond, "I'm fine, and you?"

since their icy phone call about Devon's snooping into the scholarship.

But even with parental consent, Dr. Hsu was taking a risk writing out prescriptions for Keaton students. She'd only been at the school for a month. And with the rampant prescription drug abuse that had been uncovered last semester, it was surprising that she'd offer a new medication as a solution.

Once Ms. Hadden's footsteps faded, Devon flipped open her laptop and did a search on Vericyl. The site came up instantly: images of young women of various ethnicities laughing together at a coffee shop, a family sitting at the dinner table, the mother looking especially happy and calm over her roast chicken dinner. The fine print at the bottom of the screen caught Devon's attention. *FDA Approval pending. ©Dover Industries, USA.*

Devon stared at the words. How many times had she seen the Dover, Merck, Pfizer, and Lilly brands and thought nothing of it? But the Dover on this antiseptic webpage was the Dover family she knew. The living, breathing, pregnant Maya, C.C. Tran—who was so famous for marrying Edward Dover, Junior. that she didn't need to add the "Dover" to her last name—and Edward Dover, Sr. The same Edward from Reed's journals who had arrived on the hillside with young Reed and Francis Keaton already scheming to make his fortune.

Was it a coincidence that Dr. Hsu was prescribing a Dover drug? It *was* one of the big pharmaceutical companies. Maybe Dr. Hsu was trying to play up the trauma angle and increase Devon's paranoia by deliberately prescribing a Dover drug, knowing that Devon would draw one of those silly "connections . . ."

Devon groaned. Score, Dr. Hsu. Devon had just nailed a textbook example of paranoid thinking and post-traumatic stress. Maybe she *should* think about calling her mom and taking this prescription to Nurse Reilly. If there were a pill that could stop her from posing questions of her own whirling brain, she'd be all for it.

∞

THE NEXT MORNING, THE rain finally stopped. Devon found Raven meandering along a path to class, absently eating a piece of toast. Crumbs fell from her lips. Devon felt a sudden surge to hug her. It was more than just sympathy; it was also something like camaraderie and nostalgia—camaraderie with a Keaton outsider (who couldn't care less about her morning class appearance), and nostalgia for the safe warren of the guesthouse, with her and Bodhi . . .

"Hey!" Devon called, running to catch up.

Raven raised her eyebrows while she finished chewing. Devon noticed there were dark circles under her eyes, despite the overcompensating smile.

"I've been thinking about you guys," Devon said. "I figured you'd surface when you were ready."

"It's been weird. These random meetings and people all day. And then at night, Bodhi and I just . . . it's just really quiet up there." She laughed sadly. "Shit, we'd call Priscilla back if there was anything for her to do." Raven bit the inside of her cheek and looked over Devon's shoulder, blinking back tears.

"I'm so sorry," Devon said. "Is there anything I can do?"

"Nothing for me," Raven said with a shaky sigh. "It is what it is."

"For Bodhi?" Devon hoped she didn't sound too obvious. "I mean, how's he doing with all of this?"

"Honestly, he's taking it all much harder than I am. I'll tell him you asked, but give him a few days to get his head in the right place. I gotta get to the art building before the bell." Raven gave her a quick hug and dashed away, wiping her chin with the sleeve of her hoodie.

Devon felt a glimmer of relief, and she hated herself for it.

Bodhi was just grieving, which, she reminded herself, was totally normal. She had to remember not to take everything personally.

That was, after all, the beginning of the slippery descent into paranoia . . .

Devon spotted Cleo walking with a guy across Raiter Lawn. Who was that? He didn't look immediately familiar. Tall, with blond hair—and then when a laugh erupted between them, the dimples. Of course: Fresh Blood. So Cleo had set her sights on the new dimpled addition to the hillside. Cleo caught Devon's stare and waved.

"Dev! You going to English, right?" Cleo whispered something to Fresh Blood, and he held her hand for a brief moment before jogging away.

Interesting, Devon thought as Cleo strode across the grass.

"We have English together, dork. Where else would I be going?" Devon called. The bell rang. Once Cleo was near, she lowered her voice. "And why am I only now finding out about you and Grant's new BFF, a.k.a. Whatshisname?"

Cleo linked her arm in Devon's as they hurried the last few steps to their small classroom. "Oz," she said. "His name is Oz. Ohmygod, it's crazy. I mean, crazy good. I'll tell you after class. Or better yet, let's get the hell off campus this weekend. My place in the city. We need it. Like we talked about, remember? Before Hutch's grandpa died?"

"Um . . . that could work."

Cleo stopped at the classroom door. "Stop it. I don't want to hear it. No 'we'll see.' No 'that could work.'" Cleo mimicked Devon's noncommittal voice. "You are getting cabin fever, and you're so far gone, you don't even know it."

Cleo was right. She needed to get away—from this place and all its associations.

"Okay, done. But, I'm probably going to have to visit my mom if I go into the city." She swallowed. She was still being a hypocrite. She wanted to talk to her mom both about the prescription and about the scholarship. Keaton would follow her no matter where she went.

"Fine," Cleo said. "Whatever. Just as long as you promise to have a little fun."

Devon raised her right hand. "I, Devon Mackintosh, solemnly swear to have fun with Cleo Lambert. Because I know there's no way in hell she'd ever let anything bad happen to me again under her watch."

Cleo's lips curled in a naughty smile. "Define 'bad,' *chérie*."

BETWEEN MOM'S NEEDING TO sign a permission slip, and Cleo's dad's assistant submitting the right forms, Devon was impressed any of them made it off campus at all. After Friday classes, she hurried to throw a bag before Cleo's driver arrived. She'd just about finished when her phone rang.

Bodhi.

She sat on her bed as the phone rang again and again. On the fourth ring, she answered, trying to sound cheerful but not overly so. "Hey, how's it going?"

"Hey," Bodhi said. His voice was hoarse, grim.

Devon waited for him to say something more, ask a question, anything, but that was it. After an eternity, she drew in a breath. "So—"

"Raven said—"

She laughed, and to her immense relief, he laughed, too.

"You first," she said. Better to find out if he was calling with a simple question or for a real conversation.

"Raven said you asked about me. I'm sorry I've been so MIA. It's been weird around here."

"Please don't apologize," she said. "I can't even imagine."

Another long silence.

"There's a south swell coming up from Mexico this weekend," he said. "I'm going to head down the coast, see what I can find."

"Oh," Devon said. "That sounds cool. You going alone or . . ."

She hoped he would fill in the rest, maybe even mention he had a spare seat. Only after the words had spilled from her mouth did she remember she was in the middle of packing to go away with Cleo.

"Yeah, you'd be totally bored. Besides, I need a few days away from this place. I need to clear my head, you know?"

She tried to speak, but the words caught in her throat. *I feel the same way.*

"But when I'm back, let's hang, okay?"

"Okay, cool. Have fun on your surf adventure. I'll be in the city this weekend anyways. With Cleo—"

"Devon?" he interrupted.

"Yeah?"

"If Reed hadn't . . . I mean, it was kind of good there for a minute, wasn't it? I mean, between us?"

Devon smiled so wide, she was sure he would sense it. The afternoon sunshine pouring through her window suddenly brightened. Her hand trembled as she clutched the phone.

"Yeah. For a minute."

"Okay, cool. Just wanted you to know. Our timing was kind of shitty, I guess."

"Yeah, timing." Paranoia returned full force, a cloud hiding the sunset. *Our timing* was *shitty? A past-tense thing? Was he saying that this didn't work out? Or worse, he just wants to be friends and erase the kiss.* Changing the subject seemed like the safest move.

"Hey, since I'm going into the city, want to send me our friend Isaac's address? Maybe I'll do a mini stakeout or something."

He laughed softly. "Mmmm, you sure you're not going to do something on your own that you'll regret? Or rather, that I'll regret helping you do?"

"I promise. I'll keep it risk free."

"Fine, I'll send it to you before I leave. Just . . . be careful."

"You, too," she said. "Out on the waves, I mean. You're out of practice."

Bodhi laughed again, for the first time sounding like his old self.

"Bye."

They hung up, and Devon let out a long breath. What just happened? Being nice and casual had clearly backfired. *I think I just got friend-zoned.*

THE TOWN CAR IDLING in the parking lot surely belonged to Cleo. The trunk was already popped open, so Devon tossed her duffel bag in and hopped into the backseat. She nearly screamed when someone who wasn't Cleo greeted her instead.

"Oz." Fresh Blood extended a hand with his perfect smile. "Devon, right?"

"Uh . . . yeah," she said, regaining her composure. "And you're Oz? Welcome to Keaton. Must be weird starting this time of year." She sounded like a jackass. She reached for the door handle. "Sorry, but I think I got into the wrong—"

"I'm waiting for Cleo, too, Devon," he interrupted gently. "No worries."

"Oh. Right." Devon had conveniently forgotten that part of this equation. She wanted to throttle Cleo. "Your parents named you Oz? As in, the wizard of? It's not short for something, like Osgood?"

He tapped against the window and smile. "Just Oz, as in *follow the yellow brick road.* They're suckers for musicals. Don't ask." With that, he unzipped his jacket and maneuvered around in his seat to get his arms free. The gesture felt weirdly intimate, even though Devon couldn't place why. *She* was being the rude freak, not him. "I don't know where Cleo is," he added, "but I'm getting the impression time is a little flexible in her world."

"That impression is right on." Devon attempted to smile. "So you two are . . ."

"We are raising our eyebrows together, yes," he said. "You guessed it."

He smiled back, and two deep dimples appeared. They made

Devon cringe a little. But she fought her suspicions. She was just projecting her own bad experience with dimples onto Oz. Talk about textbook . . .

The door opened. "Oh good!" Cleo cried. "I'm glad you two are finally meeting properly." Behind them, the driver slammed the trunk shut. Devon bounced in her seat from the impact. "Lemme squeeze in the middle seat there."

Oz got out of the car while Cleo dove in next to Devon. "This is going to be such a fun weekend. Two of my favorite people." Cleo nudged Oz. He wrapped an arm around her shoulder. They already looked so comfortable, a matched set.

When the hell had this even started? But Devon knew that was jealousy talking, too. She'd been in self-imposed exile for the past couple of weeks. And she longed to be that much at ease with someone. She and Bodhi had never gotten into a comfortable phase, and maybe they never would. But Devon envied Cleo's ability to absorb someone into her life so instantly. Still, as Oz smiled and wrapped his fingers around Cleo's shoulder, Devon also wondered if Cleo's ease was a liability. Just who the hell was this Oz person, anyway?

"I didn't know I was third-wheeling your drive," Devon said, fake smile intact.

Cleo sniffed. "Please, there's no third wheel this weekend. We need to catch up, and we need to have some fun. Our agenda couldn't be easier." She kicked off her boots and tucked her feet, dressed in thick socks, under her. "So where are we with everything?"

Devon glanced at Oz, who was watching her intently.

"He's up to speed. Don't worry about him," Cleo said casually.

Devon's thoughts darkened. She squirmed in the plush cushions as the car pulled out of Keaton. If Cleo trusted him, she'd trust him for now, too. Besides, she no longer had a choice. "Nothing from Maya still since the funeral. But Bodhi and Raven haven't heard anything from the Dovers, either, so maybe that's a good thing."

"Probably not. They're just working up to the next phase." Cleo squeezed Oz's knee through his jeans, her fingers lingering on his thigh. "Oz, baby, wanna tell Devon what we have planned this weekend?"

Oz smiled at Cleo. Those ridiculously cute dimples made another appearance. "Well, tonight we will be staying at the lovely chez Lambert while Monsieur and Madame Lambert are conveniently out of town."

Cleo giggled and blushed.

Oh, man, Devon groaned inwardly, *they're going to be one of those couples.*

"And then," he continued, "on Saturday afternoon, Cleo and I and you, Devon Mackintosh, will meet for lunch at the Huntington House where, I have it on good authority, C.C. Tran is also scheduled to make an appearance."

Cleo elbowed Devon. "Where we will observe, spy, sneak, and/ or bribe our way into seeing what that bitch is really up to. What do you think, Dev? You in?"

Devon tried to match their enthusiasm. "That's kind of amazing. But who's your authority on C.C.?"

Oz's dimples remained in place. "My sister is the hostess at Huntington House. She's not supposed to talk about the members or anything, but we were talking, and this little tidbit rose to the surface."

"A spy with insider information? You know I can't turn that down," Devon muttered, careful to appear grateful. Of course any leads on what C.C. was up to were welcome, but again she had the nagging thought that this was almost too perfect.

Had Cleo ever found out which school Oz transferred in from? If he had come from the city like Cleo had guessed? What were the odds he knew the Hutchins family or the Dover family? He seemed to know Grant. Being new friends was one thing, but if those two had history, Devon could only imagine what morsels of gossip Grant had passed on to Oz about Devon. The possibilities made Devon cringe.

Best just to let Cleo and Oz snuggle during the drive. Devon preferred to look out the window at the green hillsides and distant ocean, anyway. Seeing C.C. would be one thing, but from now on when Cleo wasn't looking, Devon would keep an eye on Oz as well.

CHAPTER 11

Devon jerked awake to a bony elbow in her ribs. Night had fallen, and Cleo's town car pulled up in front of her stately Nob Hill Victorian. They'd arrived. How long had Devon been asleep? It didn't matter; she wanted out. She figured it was better to give Cleo and Oz the night to themselves before lunch tomorrow.

While Oz was helping their driver with the bags, Devon shook off her sleepiness. She grabbed Cleo's arm before she could slide out. "Hey, you think your driver would take me to Berkeley? I might as well try to see my mom tonight."

"Of course. But, that's not because of us, is it? You'd have your own room here. We don't have to be so obvious all the time . . ." Cleo looked out the back window at Oz, her eyelashes at half-mast.

Devon appreciated Cleo's effort, but reasoning with Cleo would be futile at this point. "It's fine. I kind of want to sleep in my own house tonight, anyways. And we'll meet up for the super secret mission lunch tomorrow. Cool?"

Cleo winked at Devon. "Okay. But you're missing out on all the fun over here."

Thank God, Devon answered silently.

AS THE CAR DROVE over the Bay Bridge, Devon closed her eyes and imagined curling up on her mom's couch. Add a thick blanket, whatever movie she could find on cable, and pizza from Cheeseboard, and she'd be a hundred percent content. She texted Mom that she'd be there soon—and could Mom pick up whatever pizza Cheeseboard was serving today? There wasn't an immediate answer. But that was no surprise; Mom was still at work, and besides, she wasn't expecting Devon until tomorrow.

When they finally arrived at the house, Devon stood on her front steps for an extra minute. She wasn't sure what she'd been expecting, but she felt oddly joyless. It had been almost a month since she'd actually been home, yet somehow it felt like she'd hadn't been here in over a year. During winter break, she had still been in a daze about Hutch, and then came New Year's Eve. The stone steps to the green front door, the milky glass on either side of the door, the tiled roof . . . all of it felt darker, more opaque, heavier.

But she was projecting again.

Devon found the spare key in the fake rock behind the Japanese maple tree. She let herself inside and paused at the front door. When she was a kid, and her mom worked late, she was remarkably fine being alone in the house. Boogeymen, shadows, strange creaks in the night never fazed her. Silence was the problem, she decided.

She let the key clink down on the kitchen table and immediately turned on CNN and turned up the volume. Then she went through the house, flipping on lights. An old pair of sweatpants and an oversized sweatshirt were wedged into the back shelf of her closet, which Devon deemed the perfect attire for her night. By the time she had taken a hot shower and finished changing clothes, Devon felt less alone—right at the moment she heard her mom's car pulling into the driveway. The door slammed.

"Hello?" Mom called in a high-pitched voice. "Dev? I got our pizza. Welcome home."

Devon heard keys hitting the kitchen table, a pizza box thumping down, and the clatter of plates on the counter. Unable to suppress a grin, she ran. Her mother swept her into a hug and buried her nose in her hair with a muffled "I missed you."

"Me, too. It's been a month," Devon said, pulling away. Her mom pushed her hair back from her face. Devon couldn't help but notice that her eyes were pink from exhaustion; the lines in her face seemed a little deeper. Then again, being a nurse wasn't exactly a relaxed, feel-good job.

"How's the cheek?" Mom asked. "It looks like it healed nicely. No scars." She waved at the table. "Sit down. I'm going to pass out if I don't eat something. Okay?" She squeezed Devon's shoulders.

"Okay, but Mom—"

"I know," her mother interrupted softly, slumping into the chair. "You want to talk this out. I do, too."

Good. As they tore off pieces of the pizza and cracked open cold Diet Cokes, Devon started in, going from how she was still feeling weird about the New Year's Eve party and the dimpled waiter, to the feeling like Dr. Hsu was pushing the Vericyl prescription on her, to her own back-and-forth about whether or not her paranoia was founded. And then there was the question of the scholarship . . .

Her mom pushed her plate away. She leaned across the wobbly kitchen table and put a hand over Devon's. "I'm happy to talk to this Dr. Hsu if you would like," she murmured. "I don't know how I feel about her prescribing medications for you after only a few sessions, but if you're feeling a little off from your usual self, maybe it's something we should be considering."

Devon hesitated. "I know. I was thinking the same. But on the other hand, I'm not being paranoid; I'm being smart. This is so annoying. I feel like if I was a guy, I'd be taken more seriously, like all of you see me as some little girl being overly dramatic." She quickly realized that she was, in fact, being overly dramatic. She took a deep breath. "I just want some answers, that's all."

Staring into her eyes, Mom squeezed Devon's hands. "Well, I do care. Let's get you some answers. No more taking the law into your own hands, like you did with Eric Hutchins, okay? You're very smart and very capable, but you're not a superhero. Everything doesn't have to be your responsibility." She closed the distance between them and kissed Devon on the forehead, then stood. "Now help me clear the plates. You look like you're ready for some serious couch time."

DEVON FELL ASLEEP ON the couch somewhere into their third episode of *Grey's Anatomy*. She woke up a few hours later and dragged herself upstairs to her room, the old purple blanket wrapped around her shoulders. For the first time since she'd arrived, she felt at home and at peace.

At the end of the second-floor hallway, Devon saw that her mom's bedroom door was closed, but the light was on inside. Mom must have gone to sleep while reading with the light on again. But as she approached, she heard her mother whispering on the phone. Who could she be talking with at 2:15 in the morning? Devon leaned closer and listened to her mother's voice, quiet and urgent.

"That's what I told her!" her mom hissed.

Devon put her ear to the door. The wooden floorboards in the hallway let out a muffled creak.

Her mom's voice stopped suddenly.

Devon paused, holding her breath. After a long wait and silence, her mom's bedroom light clicked off.

Screw it. Devon couldn't just stand here all night, thinking paranoid thoughts. Mom was probably on the phone with one of her patients. Devon tiptoed to her bedroom but made a point to sleep with the door open.

"DEV, I'VE GOT TO get moving. Do you need a ride anywhere?"

Mom seemed distracted. They'd sipped their coffee in silence until now, and then her mom started making her to-do lists for the upcoming week. Devon figured she might as well pack up to meet Cleo back in the city.

"Yeah. To the BART. Thanks."

She left her mom to clean the kitchen and bolted upstairs. Her mom's bedroom door was closed. This might be Devon's only shot. She quickly opened her mom's door, praying that the hinges wouldn't betray her. But there was no clue, just the bed, neatly made, a stack of folded clothes on top of the white dresser, and a short stack of books next to the bed. Her mom's phone wasn't in here, and the trash can was empty.

"Gotta run, Dev!" Mom called.

Devon was careful to answer from the hallway. "One sec!"

She grabbed her overstuffed backpack and paused, taking one more glance at her mom's room before she closed the door. The top book on the stack on her bedside table stood out—only because it wasn't brand new. It was a worn paperback, the paged dyed a faded green. It reminded Devon of the paperback racks at the Berkeley library, books that had been read and handled by countless students over decades of use.

Love Story by Erich Segal. The jacket featured a cheesy, dated-looking picture of two actors embracing. They looked familiar, but Devon couldn't quite place them. They were probably old and wrinkled now. The binding was creased, the cover bent open. Devon could just make out something scrawled inside. She lifted the cover with a finger. On the first page was a penciled phone number, faded and slightly smudged. A 415 area code. Local.

Without thinking, Devon yanked out her phone and took a

quick photo. Could that belong to the person her mom was talking to last night? She'd have to try it later. And no, she was not being paranoid. She was being practical. Her mother lived alone. A caring daughter had every right to snoop.

CHAPTER 12

Huntington House felt like stepping into a time capsule. Devon had heard rumors, of course, about the swanky club built at the height of Prohibition. Black-and-white photos lined the hallways: white men with cigars, black waiters, women with cigarette holders and oversized furs draped loosely over their shoulders. There was so much political incorrectness in each photo Devon was amazed that the San Francisco cultural elite didn't protest. Then again, the current elite had probably sprung from this historic group. Grandpa might have been a racist, but he was still Grandpa . . .

Oz's sister, Zara, stood behind a wide hostess podium at the restaurant entrance. She was impossible to miss; she was the female version of Oz—stocky and blonde, complete with dimples. He and Cleo were running late, of course.

Not wanting to make small talk, Devon fled to the restroom.

Flowery sofas, dimmed sconces, perfumed lotions and soaps next to the row of sinks . . . if only she'd had a grandpa who'd been rich.

A petite Asian woman sat on a small vanity stool in front of the mirror, smoothing down her short bob. A familiar woman. Devon froze for an instant. Before the woman could glimpse Devon in the mirror, she ducked into a nearby stall. With the door closed, she might go undetected, but Devon held her breath anyways.

The woman's cell phone rang. She answered in a crisp, professional voice. "This is Jocelyn."

Devon knew that name, and she knew that voice. Dr. Jocelyn Hsu. She was *here*. At Huntington House. But why? Did she come from old San Francisco money? Did she marry a wealthy doctor or decide to join this boys' club on her own? Devon was pretty sure she hadn't seen a wedding ring on Dr. Hsu's hand. Plus, a student therapist didn't seem like the usual clientele. Devon couldn't help but smile to herself, even as her mind reeled. Seeing a Keaton faculty member out in the real world was a rarity—and a delicious one.

"Just coming out," Dr. Hsu continued. "See you in a sec."

The bathroom door closed with soft swish of air. Devon waited ten more seconds, then slipped out of her stall and followed.

Behind the podium, Devon could see Zara smiling and chattering to Dr. Hsu, clearly in hostess mode. Dr. Hsu wasn't alone now. She was with C.C. Tran.

Devon watched from inside the lobby as Zara grabbed two menus from a shelf in the podium and turned toward the dining room. C.C. Tran, in another matching outfit of skirt, blazer, and heels, was here for lunch, just as Cleo had promised she would be. Except that Cleo failed to mention that C.C.'s lunch date was Dr. Hsu.

Zara led them to a table near the window with a view of the Financial District down the hill. She pulled out a chair. Devon had to leap out of C.C.'s line of sight to avoid being spotted. Her heart thumped. She turned toward the heavy oak doors and heard a shout of familiar laughter.

Cleo burst in with Oz right behind her. Both were dressed appropriately for lunch at a stodgy club—at least more appropriately than she was—but too bad.

Devon grabbed Cleo's arm. "Stop. You can't go in. We have to leave."

She caught the door before it closed fully and tugged at Cleo and Oz before they could argue. On the front steps, with the sun shining and a brisk San Francisco breeze, she took a moment to breathe. One she felt like her feet were back on the ground in reality again, she turned to meet their baffled stares.

"Maya's mother is having lunch in there with my freaking Keaton therapist," she stated.

Cleo tilted her head, waiting for more. She didn't seem impressed. Next to her, Oz shrugged. "Whoa, talk about worlds colliding," he said.

"Thank you, *yes*, worlds colliding." Devon gritted her teeth. "Exactly."

Oz glanced at Cleo, who stepped forward. "Okay, hold up. Let's think about this for a sec. C.C. Tran has a daughter who was a student at Keaton, and by the looks of things, may even return. Dr. Hsu is the new school psychologist. Maybe they're talking about Maya?" She smiled and nudged Devon's arm. "I mean, Devon . . . this might not be about *you*, you know?"

Devon blinked at her friend. *My God.* Cleo was totally right. Worse, so was Dr. Hsu. Worst of all, Devon's paranoia was starting to scare her.

"Lemme see if Zara can help us at all," Oz said in the silence. He ducked inside the main doors.

For the first time since this weekend began, Cleo and Devon were alone.

Cleo smiled at Devon, the right side of her mouth threatening to burst into a full-on grin.

"This is not how you want to spend the weekend, is it?" Devon muttered.

"Guilty!" Cleo shrieked. She grabbed Devon's shoulders. "It's so good. He's like, *Wow, wow, like, where have you been all my life?* And Dev, it's not just sex. We've been having fun and laughing and real conversations. Holy shit. I'm not into relationships, but I don't know—" She broke off when Oz returned.

He flashed Devon a polite smile, the same sort of smile his sister had given Dr. Hsu. "There's a side entrance. Zara's going to let us in there. Come on." Oz held Cleo's hand and led them down the front steps, around the mansion to a smaller entrance flanked by garbage cans.

Zara was holding the door open when they approached. She didn't look happy; she looked annoyed—older-sister annoyed. She ushered them into the storage section of the club's kitchen. "This is kind of as much as I can help with," she whispered at Oz. "You can see them eating in the dining room through that doorway." Zara pointed toward a crowd of busboys and waiters. "See that guy with the reddish hair? He's their waiter. I'll try to flag him down, see if there's anything interesting he overhears . . ."

Devon had stopped listening. Her eyes widened. As the reddish-haired waiter carried his tray through the swinging door, a busboy passed in the other direction. One of the chefs at the stovetop yelled something in Spanish, and the busboy laughed—flashing dimples.

Devon's mouth went dry. She gripped Cleo's arm. The busboy was Eli, her waiter from New Year's Eve. "It's him," Devon said, her breath coming in irregular bursts. "Dimples."

Zara hesitated, scowling. "Are you okay? Oz, what are you doing to me, bringing these people—"

Cleo looked over her shoulder, then quickly back at Devon. Her face went white. "What do you want to do? Get out of here? Call the cops?"

Devon could only nod, her eyes pinned to Eli as he placed the last lemon wedges in his water glasses. As if feeling her gaze on him, he turned. A moment of blank confusion in his eyes quickly shifted to recognition. He flashed a brittle smile at Zara, and then picked up his tray and calmly walked into the dining room.

Cleo leaned toward Zara. "Does that guy really work here?"

"Eli? Yeah, sometimes." She whirled to her brother. "Oz, what is this about?"

"I have to get out of here," Devon said. She pushed past Cleo and out the side kitchen door. She reached the top of the stairs in time to see Eli running out the club's opulent front door—down the hill on California Street. Devon took a few steps after him but decided against it. He was too fast, and she was too scared. She turned back to Huntington House. Cleo was chasing after her, with Oz and Zara trailing behind.

"He's gone," Devon yelled.

"And now it's time for you to be gone, too," Zara snapped back.

Devon's eyes flashed to Cleo. She wasn't sure if the emotion she read was pity or fear or concern, but it didn't really matter.

CHAPTER 13

A few hours and several bus rides later, Devon arrived at 16th Street in the Mission District. Alone. Cleo and Oz had bailed on her shortly after Zara had, and Devon had let them go. Why involve them, anyway? This was her problem . . .

She knew that what she was doing was inherently stupid, but it was her only option. She couldn't face an afternoon of trying to convince Oz that Eli was her attacker. Sure, Cleo might back her story, but then what? Would he go back to his sister? She clearly wanted no part of this . . . whatever this was. Investigation? Delusion? She wanted to keep her cushy hostess job without her little brother showing up and jeopardizing it. And Devon couldn't blame her.

Once the bus had pulled away, Devon reached for her phone and brought up the address Bodhi had given her. Isaac Green lived only a few blocks away. She still didn't know his role in all this. If Eli had been spooked by Devon, maybe he would have alerted Isaac? She knew it was a reach, but this was her only chance to suss him out.

She found the buzzer outside of the Delores Street address. It had a row of dirty white buttons with names taped across the top of each: apartments A, B, C, and D. *I. Green* was scrawled in blue ballpoint above apartment A.

Devon pressed the buzzer before she could change her mind.

Now she was committed. If he didn't respond in thirty seconds, she would leave. Ten, eleven, twelve—*buzzzz!* The door unlocked.

You asked for this, she told herself. *You're the one that wanted answers.*

She wished she had some pepper spray in her bag nonetheless.

Devon made her way up the narrow wooden staircase to Apartment A. The building was another one of those old Victorian houses like Huntington House, but this one had fallen on hard times, given the neighborhood, and been split into multiple apartments. Devon wondered how the house originally looked before the chipped white paint outside and yellowing wallpaper. The wooden banister wobbled under her hands. She heard a door in the hallway above open. *Last chance to change your mind.*

She pressed on, arriving at the second-floor landing.

Isaac Green was standing at the door. She recognized his curly brown hair from the ID tag Bodhi and Raven had pulled from the catering company. Except now he had the beginnings of a mustache on his upper lip. He looked barely older than she was, barefoot and wearing jeans and a green T-shirt.

He raised his eyebrows at her, waiting for her to talk first.

"Hi, um, you're not expecting me. But you're Isaac, right?" Devon stayed near the top of the stairs. Best not to immediately walk into the lion's den.

"Yeah, that's me." He crossed his arms in front of his chest. "And you are?"

"Sorry, I'm Nora." Giving him her real name was a bad idea, right? Or did she just screw everything up?

Too late now. "I was wondering if you could help me with a few questions about the catering company you work for. It's about New Year's Eve."

Devon could swear she noticed a hint of fear flash in Isaac's eyes, but he composed himself quickly. "You might as well come in." He took a few steps back and turned, beckoning her to follow.

She smiled politely and forced her feet into his apartment.

Since he didn't seem to recognize her and didn't immediately try to kill her, Devon reasoned they were off to a good start. He smelled like that minty organic health soap that could be used to wash everything from your floor to your underarm hair. Economical and earthy: she could work with that.

The bay windows in his living room were framed in dark flaking wood. Two mismatched pillows were placed on one side of the low futon in a feeble attempt at decorating. Was this what life after Keaton and Stanford had in store for her?

No. Best to focus on the real crisis, in the real present.

"You want some water or something?" he asked.

"I'm fine, thanks. I really don't want to take up your time."

Isaac extended a hand to the futon, and she sat on the edge of it. She could feel the hard bar under the flimsy cover. He pulled the two pillows off the futon and sat cross-legged on the floor across from her. "You said something about New Year's?"

She noticed his army-green T-shirt had a spray-painted figure of a little girl reaching after a balloon. Bansky. She only knew that because Cleo's father had bought her one of the originals of that image; it had probably cost a lot more than Isaac's shirt. "Yeah, New Year's. This might sound strange, but did you work that night? On a yacht in the harbor?"

"Yes. I mean, yeah. Pretty sure I did. I'd have to look at my calendar." His eyes flitted to the window behind Devon.

"'Cause something happened to a friend of mine that night, and we've been looking into everyone who was there. And thing is . . . your ID doesn't match the person carrying it." *And bt-dubs, did you try to kill me?* Okay, she wouldn't push that far—yet. But the reaction she'd wanted, fear, was nowhere to be seen.

Isaac laughed easily and shook his head. "I knew that was going to come back and bite me in the ass," he muttered. He crossed the living room into the narrow kitchen, where beige linoleum curled up at the seams. She could hear the fridge opening and the snap of a metal cap being pried off a bottle. He leaned back into the living room, holding out a thick, round bottle of murky liquid. "Kombucha?"

"No, that's fine. Really." If this was what post-college life *was* like, she'd have to stay in college as long as possible.

He took a long sip and plopped back down on his floor pillows. "This guy gave me five thousand bucks to let him use my ID card that night. Said no one would ever know, and it wouldn't come back to me in any way."

"Five thousand bucks!" she cried.

He nodded, his eyebrows arched. "I know, crazy money, right?"

"And you took it?"

He waved around his apartment. "Wouldn't you? Five thousand dollars with no strings. Plus you get your New Year's Eve back from working for a bunch of rich assholes. Seemed like a good deal. I considered it the Christmas bonus I never got." He took a sip of his drink. "I should have known it was too good to be true . . ."

"There's nothing good about it," Devon muttered.

He glared at her. "What? Am I in trouble or something for it? Did someone rat me out to the managers?"

"What do you think?" Devon leaned back, thinking of how Dr. Hsu would draw out the answers from her in their sessions.

"He told me the only condition was I couldn't tell anyone about it."

"But you told *me*."

"It's been, like, a month, right? What's the guy gonna do? Hunt me down for telling the truth? I don't even know his name, anyway. Anyway, he seemed mellow."

Mellow. Devon scanned the bookshelves. *Life of Pi. Shantaram.* A Thailand guide for backpackers. *Eating Animals* and *The Lord of the Rings.* Isaac was probably telling the truth. He was an innocent, naïve, not-so-bright hippie incapable of imagining the worst about a stranger with a wad of cash. "Is there anything else you remember about him? Like, how did he contact you? What he maybe looked like?"

Isaac took another sip of his kombucha, considering her question. "I guess it was the day before New Year's Eve. So what's that? New Year's Eve Eve?" He smiled, but Devon couldn't find any humor in it. "I got an email asking if I was willing to swap working New Year's Eve with another waiter. A straight-up swap for another night? No, I wasn't going to miss out on holiday pay, you know? And with that crowd, tips were gonna buy my groceries for a month. So I said no dice. But the email came back, and they offered five thousand dollars. That I couldn't turn down."

Devon leaned forward. "Wait, what do you mean, 'they'?"

"I don't know. They, him, her. I'm not sure that the email came from the same guy that picked up my ID, that's all. He didn't say much, just that he'd bring my ID back later. And when I woke up the next morning, it was under the doormat, plus I was a lot richer. No harm, no foul. Isn't that what they say?"

"Are you really that stupid?" Devon cried. "What did you think someone was doing with your ID? Like, didn't any alarms go off?"

Isaac's oblivious face twisted in a grimace. "Hey, easy, sister. I let you in, didn't I? Who's to say *you* aren't some psycho?"

Devon swallowed. Point taken.

"Anyway, I figured it could have been some start-up kid wanting to get close to investors, an actor wanting to sidle up to some producer, I don't know." He grinned at her, a sudden twinkle in his eye.

"It could have been Bansky starting some neo-modern commentary on wealth and excess."

She groaned and stood. "I can tell you it wasn't fucking Banksy."

"Jeez, fine. Just a theory. And you're the one that came to me, remember?" Isaac lumbered to his feet and headed back to the kitchen. "Have a nice life, Nora. Sorry if my windfall offends you."

She paused at the front door, wincing at the fake name. "Sorry, you're right. Look, maybe you have the email the person sent you? Without going into major details, the waiter who took your place hurt someone on the yacht that night. I'm just trying to figure out who sent him there."

Isaac stood across the room, looking at Devon. She looked out the window, not willing to give up her story.

"Hurt someone? Or hurt you?" he asked softly.

Devon's throat tightened. She didn't answer. She would not cry in front of this buffoon, no matter how badly and unintentionally he'd screwed up her psyche.

"Lemme see if I can find the email. Hold on." He disappeared into his bedroom and came back with a laptop, then sat back on the floor and scrolled through emails. "There. I'll make you a hard copy."

The printer below the window near Devon churned to life. A single piece of paper rolled out. Devon looked to Isaac before grabbing it.

He nodded toward the printer. "It's yours."

"Thanks," she managed once she was certain she could talk in a normal voice. She offered a smile. "I'm sorry about snapping at you before."

Isaac's eyes flashed back to the screen, a convenient barrier. "No, I was being harsh. I had no idea something bad actually happened. I'm not, like, connected with this thing, am I?" Fear flickered in his voice as he pretended to focus on his laptop. "Like, they're not going to know I told you about them, right?"

"Nope." Devon picked up the printed paper. An email to IGMan93@gmail.com from contact@saber.com. Bodhi and Raven would be able to do something with this. "Because I was never here. I'm not Nora. Thanks for the email."

Isaac managed a sickly smile but still wouldn't look up from the bluish glow of the screen. "You're welcome, I think. The least I could do. Seriously, I had no idea. You going to be okay? You're, what, a freshman at SF State or something? If it helps, I could probably recognize the guy if I saw him again. Like, if I had to pick him out of a lineup. I'm not going to have to pick anyone out of a lineup, am I?"

"I don't think so, but it's nice to know. Take care." Devon closed the door to Isaac Green's apartment behind her before mentally adding, *And stay safe.*

CHAPTER 14

It was dark out now, and colder. In the early evening fog, Devon zipped her hoodie up to her chin. The city always tricked her into thinking it would be warmer than it was. She didn't know whether she wanted to call Cleo or go back to her mom's. At least her mom would give her some space, which she wanted more than anything. She could jump on the BART across the bay to Berkeley and be home in time for takeout dinner.

Devon headed toward 16th Street—to a coffee shop on the corner, Mission Coffee, with bright blue umbrellas over outdoor two-person tables. Her eyes flitted over a man scrolling through his cell phone. She noticed a small red mark high on his cheek, near his right eye. A burn? A birthmark? He was older, but kind of handsome; he had a nice jaw and wide lips.

As Devon passed, he looked up. His eyes quickly went back to his phone, as if he was embarrassed. Had he been checking her out? His basic black windbreaker and khaki pants looked too preppy for this neighborhood, Devon thought. Maybe he'd been a teacher at Keaton? Whatever.

She headed down the escalator into the BART station and bought a ticket just as a train pulled into the station with a piercing screech of metal on metal. Sprinting, Devon hopped through the doors just in time.

If I close my eyes, I'll fall asleep, she said to herself. She stared at her reflection in the opposite window instead. Sleep was preferable.

By the time she emerged in Berkeley, the streetlights were on, and the purple sunset was fading into the night sky. Devon tried calling her mom for a ride but only got her voicemail. She headed toward the taxi line. Maybe it was the gust of cold wind coming off the water, or just a prickling on the back of her neck, but Devon turned to look behind her.

Khaki Birthmark Guy had just emerged from the station, too. He pulled out his phone and turned his back on her, walking in the opposite direction.

Devon heart beat faster. This was a coincidence. People took the train back and forth between Berkeley and the city every day; it was entirely possible that she and this out-of-place man had a similar route. But as much as she wanted to force herself to believe that, Devon was more convinced than ever that there *were* connections. That she was not being paranoid.

The man paused at the end of the block.

Devon hurried into the taxi line while she figured out what to do next. People filed in behind her. She pulled her dark blue hood over her head. She was surrounded by dozens of onlookers; nothing bad could happen to her here. She glanced behind her again.

This time she felt the color drain from her face.

Khaki Guy was in line now, too.

As the next taxi pulled up, Devon raced from her spot and cut off an older woman about to get in the car. "I'm so sorry," she gasped. "Emergency!"

The woman stared, slack-jawed, as the cab peeled away from the curb.

Devon kept her eyes on Khaki Guy. He cut the woman off, too, and hopped in the next cab that should have also rightfully been hers.

"Excuse me, miss," the driver said, "where to?"

Devon spun in the seat. Her eyes met his in the rearview mirror; he was an elderly Hispanic man who looked long past retirement age.

"Downtown," she gasped. "Telegraph and Bancroft." She felt dizzy. *Don't panic. Don't panic.* She hunched down in her seat as the taxi pulled into traffic. Her breath stuttered in her chest. She was safe here for the moment.

She tried her cell phone. If her mom was home, she would go there. If not, she'd stay public. Her mom's cell went to voicemail. No help there. Her mom's hospital was closer to Oakland, and Devon didn't have the money to make it there.

The cab turned down Telegraph Avenue. The meter was already at $12.50. Devon had a twenty tucked in her wallet. She'd stay here until her money ran out. But after staring at the meter for another few minutes, she finally succumbed to fear. Cleo. She had to call Cleo. She'd know what to do.

Cleo picked up after the first ring. "Dev, you okay? I was worried about you."

"I think someone's following me." Devon looked behind her. She could see a white *TAXI* sign on top of a car about three cars back, but there was no way to see anyone inside. The residential section of the street gave way to the streetlights and crowds next to the UC Berkeley campus. She ducked back down in the seat. Her meter was at $16.25 now.

"Seriously? Shit. Okay, where are you? Can you get to a safe place? Is it the waiter guy?"

"It's some guy I've never seen before. I was leaving Isaac's apartment. I noticed him in the Mission, and then he was at the Berkeley station when I got off the BART. And now he's in a cab behind me."

"Who's Isaac?" Cleo asked.

Devon cringed. "He's . . . he's . . ."

"Forget it. That's not important. Um, what are you supposed to do with stuff like this? Okay, okay. Go to a public place."

"Yeah, I figured that much out." Devon poked her head up in time to see the cab passing Amoeba Records. "Stop! Stop right here."

The cab pulled over with the meter at $18.40. Devon dropped the twenty onto the front seat and jumped out, slamming the door.

"Don't hang up, Dev," Cleo said.

Devon clutched the phone tightly. She turned and saw the other cab slow to the curb, but Khaki didn't get out. "Oh, I'm not going anywhere. I want him to know I'm on the phone. I'm going into Amoeba. I think I can lose him in there if I have to. Will you come get me? I'll send you a pin of where I am."

Cleo hesitated. "On it."

Devon navigated her way through a group of panhandlers sitting among the free weekly newspapers. Posters for various bands and gigs wallpapered the front windows. *Mountain Men at Jupiter. Saturday at 8 p.m. Midnight's Shadow. Toxic Dump.* It seemed luxurious to think of having enough time to care about someone's crappy college band. She snuck a glance over her shoulder as she entered.

Khaki Guy was exiting the cab.

Devon's knees felt wobbly. At least it was crowded inside, the counters lined with bored-looking employees. a girl with a half-shaved head, the other half stringy purple hair, glared at the incoming customers as if to pass judgment. *You're not nearly cool enough to be here.* Below her a sign read *Check your bags.* Behind her were cubbies crammed with bags and purses.

The girl eyed the messenger bag slung over Devon's shoulder.

Good, let them come after me.

Devon plowed forward. Record store security seemed a much friendlier option than her khaki man. She heard a high-pitched whistle behind her, but she pushed on. She turned a quick right at the Classic Rock, Used CDs section and tucked herself behind a black-lit wall full of Bob Marley posters. A security guard in a tight black T-shirt, his biceps stretching the sleeves, turned the same corner a few seconds later.

"Miss? I'm sorry, but we need you to check your bag at the front." He extended an arm to guide Devon from her hiding place.

Khaki was near the entrance, surveying the store.

Almost on instinct Devon grabbed one of the guard's rock-solid biceps. "I'm sorry. I can't. I, uh, I need my bag." She looked up at him and realized she must really look wide-eyed and frantic. But this was no act.

"I'm going to have to ask you to leave, then," he said tersely.

He wrenched his arm free, but placed his free hand on Devon's back to steer her out. She picked up the sharp, menthol-y smell of his deodorant as they drew close to Khaki. He was as tall as the guard, but a lot less bulky. *Go on the offensive,* Devon thought. She locked eyes with Khaki, curled her lips into a faint smile, and brought them to the guard's ear.

"See that guy there?" she whispered. "He has two stolen CDs in his jacket."

The guard frowned but stepped away and headed straight toward Khaki, closing the distance between them. "Sir, do you mind coming with me?"

The man's nostrils flared as he glared at Devon. But the guard was between them now, blocking his path. That was all Devon needed. She bolted out the door and didn't stop. Outside she crossed Telegraph. She almost burst into tears when she noticed the dingy red-and-white striped awning over Moe's Books. She knew

Moe's. Multiple floors of bookshelves she could hide behind. She shot a glance behind her as she dashed inside—but Khaki hadn't managed to exit. The guard still had him. There was no way he'd seen her come in here.

On shaky legs, Devon clambered up the narrow staircase to the second floor, slid to the floor behind the Classics section, and sent a pin to Cleo. Hopefully Cleo would find her before Khaki could.

I'm not paranoid, she kept repeating to herself, over and over during the endless wait for her friend. *I'm not paranoid.*

IT TOOK SOME CONVINCING on Cleo's part to get Devon to come down the steps, let alone leave the bookstore. Oz was circling the block in her car.

"What if he's out there? He'll see me. I don't want him to know where I live," Devon said. She gripped the bookshelf in front of her, suddenly convinced that staying in the bookstore was her best option.

"You can't stay here, Dev," Cleo said as gently as possible. "I'm trying to help." So funny and ironic, wasn't it? Cleo was using the same damn patronizing peer counseling-speak Devon had used on her only three months earlier during their sessions. "You're starting to freak out the bookshop people. Come on."

A wary employee, a plump middle-aged guy, was waiting at the bottom of the stairs. Devon tried to muster an apology as Cleo escorted her past him, but the words never made it out. Instead, Devon made sure to look in every direction. No sign of the khaki guy, but she knew that wasn't the end of it. She'd been followed. There was no denying it. Someone was trying to scare her, or worse.

Cleo opened the passenger door to her mother's new Tesla, and Devon quickly sank as low as her seat would allow.

Oz smiled at her from the driver's seat. "You had us worried there, Dev," he said.

Cleo scooted into the backseat. His smile dropped when he

traded looks with her in the rearview mirror. "Just drive, Oz," she muttered. "Let's just go up MLK for a little bit. Put some distance between us and this place." She sighed loudly. "*Merde, merde, merde . . .*"

"No," Devon said. She sat up straight. "I want to go home. I need to be home."

Oz traded looks with Cleo again in the rearview mirror. What had they been saying about her after she'd abandoned them at Huntington House? Who cared? If they thought she was crazy, they'd keep her safe. That was her strategy, after all.

"Dev, you sure you don't want to stay in the city with us tonight?" he offered, "We'll go back to Keaton first thing tomorrow morning. It'll be good for you to be around friends."

"Friends?" she snapped. "We've known each other, what, thirty-six hours, Oz? You're not really in a position to decide what's good for me or not, huh?" Devon slid her left hand over her seat belt buckle. On second thought, screw safe. She could hop out at the next red light.

Cleo glared at her. "Dev, chill out. Oz is just trying to help. Remember, he's the one that got us into Huntington House."

Devon closed her eyes. Cleo was right. Being a bitch wasn't helping, either. "I know. Really, Oz, I appreciate what you're doing, especially since we really do barely know each other. I'm sorry. I just need to be home."

DEVON HAD NEVER FELT such relief as she did when she spotted her mom's car in the driveway. Cleo made a point to walk Devon to the door. Her mom answered quickly.

"Is everything all right? I didn't think I'd see you until tomorrow," she said.

Devon smiled weakly and stepped inside. She was too exhausted to answer.

"It was a rough day," Cleo explained. "Dev will tell you, but she wanted to stay here. You're going to be here tonight, aren't you?" Cleo lowered her voice. "I think she just needs some mom time tonight."

"I can hear you, okay?" Devon croaked. She whirled around. "I'm not a damn toddler. And Dr. Hsu is right; I'm clearly in shock or suffering post-traumatic stress or something. But there are a few things I can say that are true. Period. Someone followed me today. And Eli is working at Oz's sister's club where Dr. Hsu—yes, that same well-meaning Dr. Hsu—was having lunch with Maya's evil mom. That's not a fucking coincidence. How am I the crazy one here? Doesn't anyone else see it?"

Neither Cleo nor Mom responded. Oz appeared in the doorway, grinning uncomfortably. *Jesus,* Devon thought. Where did he come from, anyway?

"Oh, baby, we see it. We just want to help." Her mom crossed the room and wrapped Devon into a warm hug.

It was only then that Devon finally allowed herself to cry.

Once the tears stopped coming, once Cleo and Oz had awkwardly departed, once Mom had finally let her go, Devon trudged up stairs and fell into bed. She'd fall asleep with her clothes on, no doubt. But first she'd check her phone. No missed calls, no friendly messages. She didn't really feel like talking to anyone, anyways, except one person who might be able to make her feel better.

She texted Bodhi: hi. Can u talk?

There was no reply.

CHAPTER 15

"So here's what we're going to do. I'm going to call this Dr. Hsu and get her side of the story about this Vericyl thing. But if she makes a convincing argument, then this is something we should really consider. I'm worried about you carrying an inordinate amount of stress on your shoulders."

Devon nodded in the passenger seat of her mom's idling car, her eyes on Cleo's house and the town car in the driveway. She realized that this was the very last place she wanted to be. But given that it was Sunday morning and she needed a ride back to Keaton, she didn't have a choice.

"Honey?" her mom prodded.

"I would say it's probably the right amount of stress considering everything."

Mom sighed. "There's a woman at work whose husband is a

cop. I'm going to ask her if I can ask him a few questions. See if there is any way the police can help. Until then, I'm sure you're safe at Keaton." She kissed Devon's forehead and smiled, her eyes searching Devon's for an equal response.

Devon swallowed the lump in her throat. "Okay, thanks."

"I love you, Dev."

"You, too," Devon answered. But the words were empty, a reflex. She hopped out and headed toward the waiting town car, not even bothering to wave as her mom sped off.

Oz jumped when Devon opened the back door. "Shit," he said so quickly it sounded like a sneeze. He laughed as Devon scooted into the soft cushions. "Sorry, just didn't hear you pull up."

"I get it. It's been a jumpy weekend." Devon smiled at Oz, a peace offering.

He opened his mouth but was interrupted by his phone. He frowned at the caller ID and clicked the ringer off. Streaks of red worked their way up his neck and onto his cheeks. He was blushing about something. The phone buzzed again, and this time, Devon sneaked a peek at the caller ID. Nikki, a cute blonde. Oz shoved the phone back in his pocket.

"Your mom or dad?" Devon asked, pretending to stare out the window. "Welcome to Keaton. The Sunday-morning parent call cannot be escaped. Even when you're off campus."

"Huh? Oh, yeah. Right." Oz laughed clumsily.

Devon resisted the temptation to laugh out loud. So Oz *was* too good to be true. And he *was* hiding a secret. A very typical, stupid, new-hot-guy-at-school secret. No wonder he was being extra chivalrous with his latest conquest. She wondered if Cleo knew about Nikki. But this was not her business. Besides, after the way Devon bitched at Oz yesterday, she was sure Cleo wasn't interested in hearing Devon's theories on the Oz-secret front.

Devon checked her own phone. Still nothing from Bodhi. She

tried to hide her disappointment. She had reached out to him last night in a moment of weakness, hoping that he would at least respond with a basic *hi* back. It seemed he was purposely creating space between them. *That's fine,* she thought. *But I'm not going to call him, text him, email, anything when I get back.* She'd wait for him to contact her first.

No matter how much she wanted to tell him about her discoveries this weekend.

It took Cleo another twenty minutes before she finally finished packing and had their driver load the car. She managed to bring back to school at least three times as much as she left with for the weekend. New clothes, shoes, hats that had been buried in her closet at home, makeup samples from her mom's gift bag collection—all of it had to be smashed and wedged into the trunk.

Then the kissing and pawing began.

As they pulled away, Devon's phone buzzed. A text from Raven, asking if she wanted to get an early dinner together in Monte Vista. *Anything to escape the town car from hell,* Devon thought.

TWO HOURS LATER, CLEO seemed even more eager to part ways than Devon. For a moment, Devon felt a pang of guilt as the driver fished her bag out from the overstuffed trunk. The wind in Monte Vista was strong and frigid, but Devon hesitated. Once the driver was back inside, she knocked against the rear window. It rolled down.

"I'm sorry, Cleo, about everything this weekend," she apologized.

Cleo gave her a half-smile. "Nothing to be sorry for."

"We're cool, right?" Devon asked.

"Dev, I love you. We're cool. I'm sorry this weekend was so dramatic—" Cleo sighed. "See you on the hill."

Devon nodded as Cleo rolled her window back up. At least she'd understood enough to cut Devon some slack. But it wasn't her role to be Devon's protector. She wasn't responsible for what had happened on the yacht—or after.

RAVEN WAVED FROM HER booth in the back, and Devon stiffened slightly.

Bodhi was sitting in the booth as well, his back to the front door.

Devon wished she could slowly back out of the deli and catch up with Cleo's car. Of course she knew that this was a possibility. Maybe that's what she'd secretly been hoping for when Raven texted, but right now, she didn't feel sturdy enough to be the cool, calm *friend* the Elliots knew.

"We ordered for you, sorry," Raven said. "We were starving."

She wrapped Devon into a big hug. Bodhi scooted out from the booth, and before Devon could decide whether or not it was appropriate to hug Bodhi, he was hugging her, too.

"How was your weekend?" He sat back down and left a seat open for Devon to sit next to him. Devon nudged Raven and slid in next to her. "I didn't surf, if that's what you mean." She could hear the biting sarcasm in her voice, but she didn't care. While Bodhi was off being one with the ocean, Devon had been stalked. And he couldn't even return a text.

Bodhi and Raven glanced at each other. He took a bite of his pastrami sandwich before answering. "I just saw that you texted. I didn't turn my phone on for the last two days. I think it was just what I needed, but looking at you now, I think that might have been a mistake . . ."

Devon hated her own selfishness, but she couldn't control it. "I saw Isaac, for starters," she mumbled.

"What?" Bodhi and Raven gasped.

And with that, the story tumbled out in a messy jumble: seeing Dr. Hsu at lunch with C.C., spotting Eli working at the Huntington House, her visit with Isaac, the eerie chase into Berkeley, her mom's promise to talk to her cop friend. Bodhi and Raven were both silent, their food growing cold on their plates.

"Holy shit," Raven finally muttered. "How are you not a total wreck right now?"

"Who says I'm not?" Devon laughed, but it sounded forced, and she knew it.

"Unfortunately, it sounds like the common thread here is that the police can't get involved." Bodhi poured more ketchup into a puddle next to his fries. "Nothing really happened, and we don't even know what we're after."

"Nothing really happened, huh?" Devon snapped back.

Bodhi didn't respond, but his blue eyes turned frigid.

"Okay," Raven began, "we're all a little spent, for all kinds of reasons. We have a few options. One, if Eli works at Huntington House legally, we can find more info on him. Two, Isaac said he got an email. We can probably try to get into that account, trace it back to where it was sent from . . ." Her voice trailed off. "But."

"But," Bodhi echoed. He and Raven traded a look.

"But what? Yes to both of those ideas. What's the 'but' about?" Devon asked.

"Now that we have property and assets and stuff," Raven said, "it's . . ."

"Tricky," Bodhi finished. "We've been advised to be upstanding citizens and all that entails."

Once again, Devon felt like a jerk for missing the obvious. In the last few weeks, Bodhi's and Raven's life had been irrevocably changed. Having money and property now meant that they had something to lose. Something that lawyers and advisors would be watching closely.

"You two, upstanding citizens? Hold on, let me get my head around that one. It might take a minute," Devon joked.

Bodhi threw a fry across the table, hitting Devon's cheek. His eyes seemed to melt, and for a second she forgot she was mad at him. She turned her attention back to her own untouched grilled cheese.

"I'm sure we can hide our IP," Raven said, almost to herself.

"Let's do the mouse trap," Bodhi agreed. "We send a spam email, see if they ping us back, and find the source IP from there. It might take a bit longer, but we break fewer laws."

Devon blinked a few times. "Really? You're sure?"

Bodhi reached across the table and patted her shoulder. The gesture was casual, easygoing, brotherly. "Hey, we're glad you're back in one piece. Next time, we're going with you. Friends don't let friends investigate alone."

Devon tried to smile back. But inside, every organ, every muscle, every electric current of brain activity cringed.

Friends.

BACK IN HER ROOM, Devon dumped all her books out of her backpack and onto her bed. Four hours of studying stared her in the face. She fought the urge to shove all the books onto the floor and crawl under her comforter for the rest of the night. Her body seemed to creak as she flipped open her laptop. A perfect end to a perfect weekend . . .

There was a new email waiting. Had Raven gotten a response from Isaac's emailer already?

Devon frowned at the Keaton school address. She didn't recognize the name of the sender, though. And Keaton was misspelled. *Keeton.edu.*

What the—? She opened the email, and a picture popped up on her screen. It was of Raven and her leaving the Monte Vista Deli, Devon's napkin-wrapped sandwich in one hand while she slid her arm into her jacket with the other. Raven was fishing her car keys from her straw purse. That was just a half hour ago.

Whoever had followed Devon in San Francisco wasn't content to let it stop there.

CHAPTER 16

Session #3: Devon Mackintosh
Monday, January 28, 2013

Dr. Hsu's lipstick was distracting. It was a deep purple shade Devon had never seen her wear in session before—or even around campus. Devon pictured her sitting in front of the bathroom mirror at the Huntington House before answering her phone. *This is Jocelyn.*

The words froze in Devon's mind, at once humanizing her therapist and exposing her deceit. Devon glared at the purple semi-circle Dr. Hsu's lipstick left along the rim of her teacup.

"How are you feeling today?" Dr. Hsu asked.

Devon shrugged. She was more curious where Dr. Hsu would try to take the session. Let her *really* fill in the blanks this time.

"I spoke with Nurse Reilly," Dr. Hsu continued. "It seems you haven't filled the Vericyl prescription. Have you had a chance to speak with your mom about it?"

"A little." Devon fought the urge to speak further, but

couldn't. "Funny thing about Vericyl. Did you know that it's a Dover drug?"

"I'm not sure I follow." Dr. Hsu's smile started to flatten at the edges.

"Dover Industries. Maya Dover, the pregnant Keaton student. Her mother's been around campus picking up her assignments, packing up her dorm room. The Dovers are kind of a big deal around here. I'm sure you've at least heard of them."

"Oh, I wasn't aware it was the same Dover family." Dr. Hsu dropped her eyes and sipped her tea.

"Weren't you?" Now Devon focused the same pleasant smile on Dr. Hsu. She would not be convinced this was all a silly mistake, another coincidence to laugh off.

"So because of this Dover connection, you're not interested in trying the prescription? This is one of the things we were working on, Devon—"

"No, it's one of the things *you're* working on. I might as well be a slab of paranoid, post-traumatic meat."

In spite of the interruption, Dr. Hsu's professional smile returned. Devon had to hand it to her; she was unflappable. "Vericyl can help with these feelings," she said. The condescension in her voice made Devon's fingers curl into fists.

"What's it matter to you if I take this thing or not? You're just here for the semester, aren't you? You won't even be here long enough to see if it works."

Dr. Hsu shook her head. "I may be here longer."

"I see what you did there: careful avoidance of specifics, nothing that you have to actually commit to. Except you haven't answered my question. What's your personal stake in all this, Dr. Hsu? Are the Dovers paying you to get all of us on Vericyl? Or is it just me?"

Finally she'd struck a nerve. Dr. Hsu's smile evaporated. "I don't appreciate your tone, Devon. Maybe we should reschedule for when you're feeling a little less combative." She sat up straighter and smoothed the blanket over her lap.

"There's no need to reschedule. We're probably good here." Devon stood up to leave.

"Hold on a second. We're not finished yet. You're required to complete five sessions with me."

Devon returned her steely glare. "And you're required to provide a safe, confidential, therapeutic environment. It says so in the Keaton Student handbook. I'm sorry, Dr. Hsu. I don't feel safe if I'm being lied to. I can talk the talk, too. And I can't continue if these parameters aren't being adhered to."

Dr. Hsu almost looked amused. "Devon, please have a seat. Let's discuss this rather than jumping to conclusions. I don't know where you're getting these ideas."

"Ask your friend C.C. Tran," Devon replied. "She might know. You can discuss it over lunch at Huntington House."

The last image Devon had of Dr. Hsu was of her teacup slipping from her fingers and spilling onto the floor. The door slammed on the session room as if in a dream; Devon didn't even hear it. The next thing she knew, she practically skipping down the cement hallway toward the dining hall. Her heart was beating fast. She hadn't exactly planned on calling Dr. Hsu out like that, but at this point she had nothing to lose. Not even as the old doubt and questions slithered into her mind . . .

What if Cleo was right? What if Dr. Hsu and C.C. had never even spoken about Devon? What if Dr. Hsu had other reasons for denying knowing the Dovers? Maya was *pregnant*. That was serious, and that was real. So now what? What if Dr. Hsu reported Devon to Headmaster Wyler as being out of control?

In the end, it didn't matter. It just meant they'd watch her even more closely. As closely as whoever had taken those pictures last night of her and Raven. Whether Dr. Hsu was involved or not, being passive was no longer an option.

September 4, 1942

I'm going to have to be careful to not let anyone
know about this diary. Just last month, the Man-
hattan Project was announced. All of us were issued
new sets of IDs and uniforms. We're supposed to
be working with the Army now, more than we were
before.

They say it's for our safety.

We've made progress with our metals with various degrees of magnetic abilities. A few days ago,
we sent a crate of prototypes of shell and bomb
casings to New Mexico. It was a milestone in our
work to finally have something that Dr. Keaton
was satisfied with. He has very high standards. He
says it's because Dr. Oppenheimer's standards are
even higher. We celebrated the accomplishment with
a bottle of champagne, a rare extravagance for
Dr. Keaton.

Athena and Hana have been so supportive. Hana
planted three pine trees in our names to celebrate.
She said it was a tradition in her family to plant a
new tree for a milestone. Her parents' back yard
is lined with the pine trees from each of her birth-
days.

That night, after the champagne and the wine
had been flowing for a few hours, I had an idea.
The Army engineers were on the hillside earlier
in the day, pouring another wall of concrete for
the new bunker overlooking the water. There was
so much moisture in the air, I figured we still had
time. I didn't tell them what we were going to do.

Eddie was still gloating about our work and how

we were going to be rich, the three of us—"the three trees," he called us—on our future projects. He talked about us having a lab in Berkeley where we could continue our work. He was so excited to sell our patents to his friends at Merck and wanted to start his own pharmaceutical company, and it would make all of us rich.

I noticed Keaton was smiling politely as Eddie spoke. But I don't think he ever wants to leave this mountain.

I steered everyone to the new bunker. The concrete was still wet.

As Athena held up the lantern, I found a branch and carved an outline of three trees into the wall, just like Hana's trees. Keaton and Hana were standing behind me, and Keaton put his hand on my shoulder. "We're going to do great work here," he said. "This hillside will know we were here." He read my mind, because he stepped forward and pressed his hands into the back wall of the bunker. We all left our handprints in the wall that night.#

The bell rang for the end of second period. Devon had five minutes to get to English. She flicked her thumb across the page corners in Reed's diary. What was so important in here that Reed wanted her to find out? There had to be more than a basic history lesson in these pages. On the other hand, Reed wasn't exactly in the best mental state when he gave it to her. What was it he had said?

Footsteps? 'You'll need it to follow our footsteps.'

Devon flipped the brittle pages again. Stories and scientific jargon were written throughout. What about these stories would help her follow in Reed's footsteps? Did he mean that literally or figuratively? Raven and Bodhi were in more of a position to carry on

Reed's legacy than Devon, since he'd given them everything of his. Were these pages somehow a guide to the Keaton hill itself?

She held the book upside down and shook the pages. Nothing fell out. The paper looked normal; there was no secret treasure map to be found if she held the pages by candlelight, was there? That would be hard to believe.

Devon laughed at herself. Was she seriously thinking there was an "X marks the spot" map somewhere in this book? *Give it up, Devon. Reed wasn't a pirate. He was a sweet old man.*

Devon flipped to the back of the book. At least she should know when he last wrote in it. Maybe that would help.

The last page stuck to the back cover. She shook it, but the paper didn't budge. She felt along the edges; it seemed to be evenly attached in each corner as if done on purpose rather than a result of age. She could feel the slight bulge of another sheet of paper underneath.

Devon slowly wedged a ruler through the sticky border. She hoped that the entire back cover wasn't about to fall off.

The last page came unstuck. Folded behind it was another piece of paper, thicker, with a coarse grain. Devon unfolded the sheet and found a blurry drawing of charcoal lines smudged together across the page, and from below the charcoal emerged two crisp hand-prints.

They all left their handprints in the cement in the bunker that night.

This must have been a charcoal rubbing from one set of those handprints. It was one thing to read Reed's stories, but these hands, detailed with wrinkles and callused palms, made Reed's words more than real. And the bunker, Devon realized—once new and full of purpose from Reed's perspective—was a place as familiar to her as any on campus.

The Three Trees' bunker was the Palace.

∞

THERE WAS NO WAY Devon could sit through English now. She had to know if the handprints were at the Palace. Years of rain, erosion, cigarette burns, and graffiti had all but destroyed the walls and surrounding hillside. But the possibility that hidden in the dirt-encrusted, glass-riddled cement were pairs of handprints from the school's founders was too much for her to resist. It ultimately drove her to cut class, hurry back to her dorm, and pull on a pair of rain boots.

The rain was lighter in the morning, but the dirt trail was still slippery with mud rivulets running down the hillside. Slipping away in the drizzle had been easier than expected. Everyone had their head down, hurrying to their next classes. Devon gripped the crumbling edge of the bunker and sloshed a foot through the puddle in the middle of the cement floor.

Hutch had died right here.

She pushed the image out of her mind. She squinted, trying to rewind the setting further back to a time when the bunker was still freshly poured cement. She ran her fingers along the wall, feeling the even groove between each block. The handprints would have remained. She didn't believe they could have faded into a perfectly smooth wall. The bunker hadn't been used since the end of World War II, so it seemed unlikely that anyone had put the time or effort into repaving, either.

But the handprints weren't there.

She felt along the outside walls, the curved, shell-shaped top hanging low over the bench and disappearing into the hillside above. How much had the hillside shifted since Reed had stuck his hands in the wet cement?

Frustration gnawed at her. What the hell was she doing here, anyway? Across the mountainside, Devon could see Reed's grapevines leading the way up to his guesthouse, everything tinged gray in the rain. Bodhi was probably working there right now. If she hurried, she could probably be back on campus by lunchtime before anyone really knew she was missing. Bodhi would know where to look for the handprints. No matter how upset she was with him for abandoning their mini-relationship, she needed his help. They *were* friends.

CHAPTER 17

Bodhi was clearly confused to see Devon on his doorstep in the middle of a rainy school day. He looked behind her as if expecting to see Raven climbing out of her car. When she didn't appear, his brow knit. "Uh . . . you alone?"

"Just me," Devon said with a shrug. "Can I come in?"

"Yeah, sure. Of course." Bodhi stepped aside, and Devon headed straight for his computer. "Do I want to ask why you're here? Last I heard, you guys still had classes on Mondays. Not that I pretend to understand what goes on at that school."

Devon pulled Reed's diary from her jacket pocket and dropped it onto Bodhi's desk. "Reed gave me this."

Bodhi's eyes widened. The jokiness vanished. He sat and began to flip through the delicate pages, his strong fingers treading lightly.

"It's his diary from when he and Athena moved to the hill,"

Devon explained. "They were scientists during World War Two. A bunker was built, and they put their handprints in the wall there. I thought it was the Palace, but now I'm not sure . . ." Her voice trailed off.

Bodhi's jaw twitched. This was emotional for him in ways she hadn't counted on. *No wonder he wants to be friends. Why can't I be a better friend to him?* He looked up, his eyes moist.

Devon unfolded the charcoal rubbing of the handprint. "I think we're supposed to find this. I don't know why, but it just seems important to trace Reed's steps. It was actually the last thing he said to me. He repeated it a bunch of times. 'Follow in our footsteps.' I figured you might know what to do."

Bodhi looked between the drawing and the hillside out their window. "Hold on." His lips made a popping sound, opening and closing as he typed at his computer. "World War Two, you said? Any idea which year?"

"1942. He said the Army built it then." She stood behind Bodhi, watching in awe as he blew through one screen after another. Up popped the site for the Army Corps of Engineers. "You think the Army will have those records?"

"Blueprints, I'm hoping." His eyes stayed glued to the screen.

Devon leaned closer. She could smell the coconut now, that faint suntan lotion scent Bodhi always had. "And they just make that stuff available to the public?" she asked.

"Meh. There's a Freedom of Information Act thing I could fill out, but that takes weeks. Easier just to get in there and get what we need. Here. I think this is it."

Bodhi pressed PRINT and spun in his chair. Feeling light-headed, Devon straightened so he wouldn't bump into her. Pages of diagrams started spewing out from his printer. Devon's eyes latched onto one, an overview of the entire bunker, and she grabbed it before it was buried in the growing pile.

"There're two levels," she said.

Bodhi reached for the diagram, his hand lightly brushing Devon's lower back. Her breath caught in her chest for a split second.

But Bodhi didn't think anything of it, of course. What they were doing necessitated intimacy. It was an accident. Friends could accidentally bump one another. It didn't have to mean anything.

"You know what this means," Bodhi said, his eyes slits as they roved the complex array of schematics. "It means that generations of Keaton students either didn't know about the second level of the bunker, or they kept it a secret." He glanced up with a smirk. "How many kids do you know at Keaton who can keep a secret?"

Devon almost laughed out loud. She studied the diagram again. The Palace as they knew it was only the top level. Below it there was another lookout point with a small interior space built inside the mountain.

"The room's only, like, six by eight feet," Bodhi said, squinting.

"Amazing," Devon murmured. Her breath came fast. "There's a room, Bodhi. An effing *room*. I mean, anything could be in there. Army supplies. Reed could have left stuff there. The handprints have to be on that wall!" Devon realized her eyes were so wide, she hadn't blinked in a minute. *Blink. Breathe. Blink again.*

But Bodhi was just as excited. He nodded vigorously, spurring her on. "I know. If Reed's diary told you to go there, then there's definitely something there."

Devon fell back onto the futon. She pulled her hands through her hair, imagining the possibilities of buried treasure. Or whatever was hidden there. It was treasure of some sort, definitely, because it was important enough to keep hidden from the Keaton School and the Dover family, the branches of the other two trees.

"We have to go," Bodhi said. "ASAP. Can we go today?"

"No, no, no. We have to be smart about this. Teachers sweep it at least once a day, looking for weed smokers. We get busted down there, everyone will know about the bunker. But it's too dangerous to go at night."

"Maybe."

Bodhi stepped to the nearby closet. The doors slid open, revealing shelf after shelf of equipment: paper, computer cords, and petri dishes. *Classic Bodhi,* Devon thought. Only those he trusted most could see the science geek hidden behind the surfer façade.

"Dammit," he said.

"What are you looking for?"

"Binoculars. I want to see if we can see it from here."

"You're not serious, are you? Between the two of us, I'm rarely the genius. But come here." She crossed the room to the large windows overlooking Reed's vineyard. The hill sloped down and curved out of sight into a valley, then reemerged with the Keaton campus on the other side. Devon held up her cell phone camera and zoomed in. "There's an app for that, dude," she joked.

Bodhi laughed and shook his head. "Why do I feel old all of a sudden?"

"See?" Devon held up the phone. Bodhi moved behind her to look over her shoulder. She scanned the Keaton hillside, moving the camera along the path she took to the Palace. All of a sudden, she felt Bodhi's hand on her waist. Devon flinched, but reminded herself that he was probably not aware of what he was doing. It felt absent, hanging there. Didn't it? She shifted her weight onto her left foot to try to subtly shake his hand off.

Bodhi's breath was in her ear now. He reached up and pulled a strand of her hair off her neck. Before she knew it, he was kissing her neck.

"Okay, what the hell?" Devon whispered, her voice shaky. She felt her cheeks going hot. She spun and faced him. "I thought you wanted to be friends."

His cheeks were flushed, too. "I do. I did. I just . . . did I say that?"

"Yes, you totally said that. You friend-zoned me, and I get it, with everything that's going on. I was ready to walk away from that possibility and be your friend. But you can't get all touchy-feely whenever you want. I don't know what this is."

Bodhi stood across from her, his chest heaving. He ran a hand over his dreads. "I wanted to give you space. Or I mean, I guess I needed some space, and I didn't expect you to wait around. Shit, I messed this all up, didn't I?"

She shook her head. "No. I did. And I'm doing it now, putting myself first ahead of you. But listen. You and Raven help me so much, do you really think I couldn't handle being there for you? Even if it meant waiting a little bit?"

Bodhi stepped forward and pulled Devon into a kiss before she could react. Her arms flailed by her sides for a second, but he gripped her closer, tighter, and she allowed her hands to land on his shoulders.

Finally he pulled away and opened his eyes. For the first time, she noticed the small flecks of brown in that sea of turquoise. She smiled, and he sighed.

"Thank you," he whispered. He kissed her forehead and hugged her against his chest. Devon's eyelids fluttered closed. She let her chest rise and fall in time with his. There was more to say, more she needed to do, but right now, this was where she was meant to be. It had been worth the wait.

THE SECOND RAVEN SAW the handprint rubbing, she wanted in.

Devon had taken a seat in the back of the dining hall during lunch, pulling her hoodie up over her head so as not to draw attention to herself. But before that, just to cover her bets, she went straight to Mr. Kramer and told him that she had been feeling feverish all morning. Yes, for the first time in her Keaton career, she'd accidentally slept through class. Of course he bought the lie; she wasn't one to make excuses. He let her slide with the understanding that she would catch up on the missed lesson. Good thing she'd always played by the rules ever since she and a certain boy had broken them one night before freshman year . . .

Hutch. It all came back to Hutch. But for the first time ever, she knew she could let him go and still treasure his memory.

Now she had business to attend to. At her table with Raven, Devon was careful to cough in case anyone spotted her and doubted her sick claim.

Raven ran her fingers across the aged butcher paper as if it were some magical artifact, as if not believing it was real.

"So Reed just left this in his diary?" she asked.

"Kind of. It was glued to the back cover."

"Awesome." Raven held up the sheet to the light. "So the real question is: What's the big deal with this handprint place? This is more than a memento."

Devon slid the paper in front of her. "Bodhi found the design plans. There's a room in the bunker I think we're meant to find. We just need to figure out the best time to get down there."

"I'm down for anything," Raven said.

"I know. You're fearless."

Raven's gaze drifted back to the paper. Devon opened her mouth, then closed it. For now, it seemed better not to tell Raven about the stalker photos. Fearless or not, Raven didn't deserve that added worry. Besides, they were safe here.

CHAPTER 18

Saturday seemed the best day to for their bunker mission. Most of the Keaton sports teams had games off campus—which meant fewer faculty members on patrol. Bodhi parked their Range Rover as close to the Palace as he could, a few large rocks wedged in front of the wheels for extra security. He carried a backpack full of tools, complete with thick suede construction gloves for each of them.

"What are these for?" Devon asked. She and Raven tried to stifle a giggle as they slipped the gloves on. They looked like oven mitts with fingers.

"This hill gets pretty steep. Figure we'd need something else to hang on to." Bodhi was all business. He pulled at a coil of metal cable attached to the front of the Rover. "If we hang onto this as we go, we should be okay." He carried the cable down to the edge of the Palace. The three stood on the farthest cement ledge. Devon peered down at the brush-filled abyss below.

"I don't see the lower ledge," Raven said. "Shouldn't it be there?"

"It's in the plans, so it's definitely here." Bodhi pulled an extra loop of the cable around his hand. Devon lay flat on the ground and smoothed her hands along the cement ledge. She could see bushes and dirt below, but no other cement lookout like the plans had detailed.

"Do you think if we dropped over this, we'd land on the balcony?" She turned up to Bodhi, who'd begun making his way down the hill.

"Maybe. I just don't like the idea of our feet leaving the ground when we don't know what we're landing on."

"Better listen to Mr. Precaution over here," Raven said.

She extended a hand to help Devon up. With Bodhi leading the way, they inched farther down the hillside, each of them sliding gloved hands down the taut cable. Soon Devon was perpendicular to the sloping hill. Anxiety pricked at her. What if the lower balcony had been completely covered by the shifting hillside? What if there was no way into Reed's secret room?

"There's something over here," Bodhi grunted. He reached for a tangle of ivy wrapped around a tree and was suddenly standing upright. He stomped his foot on the ground and smiled. "This is it."

"Whee!" Raven yelled as she leaned and pulled the cable—and Devon with it—toward Bodhi. Bodhi wrapped the cord around the tree stump and helped them to level ground.

Hidden in the shadow of a nearby redwood, Devon could now make out the back wall of the hidden second level. Dirt was piled in a mound against the bottom of the wall, and dusty cement arched above. She didn't hesitate. Grabbing a nearby stick, she started digging the packed dirt away from the wall. Once it was gone, she tossed the stick aside and ran her hands along the wall's flat surface.

She could feel the indentations of the handprints. Her heart leapt. This was it!

"Here, try this," Raven said. She pulled a bottle from her backpack and poured water along the top of the wall.

Five pairs of handprints were instantly visible. Small initials were carved below each: HK and FK were next to a pair of prints to their left, ED below a chubby set of prints to their right, and in the middle, RH and AH. Reed and Athena Hutchins. Raven ran a hand over the handprints on the left side. "Francis Keaton, but who's the H?"

"That's his wife, Hana," Devon murmured.

"What happened to her?" Raven asked. "Wouldn't she have a building or something named after her at school?"

Devon shrugged. "Don't know. Maybe she left before the school was built. She might have had some trouble here, being Japanese."

Bodhi dug his fingers into a groove in the wall between Reed's and Edward's handprints. "There's something else . . ." He pulled a crowbar from his backpack.

"Jeez, where you been hiding that?" Raven laughed.

"What? I came prepared," Bodhi grunted as he jammed the crowbar into the crevice. It didn't budge.

"Maybe that's not the way in," Devon said. She turned and took in the view. The trees below weren't tall enough to obscure the Pacific Ocean. But now was not the time for sightseeing. She scoured the platform and caught a glimpse of rusted red metal: a hinge.

"Look." She knelt down and wiped away the dirt. The metal continued toward the back wall.

Bodhi used the crowbar to scrape along the lines of the hinge, and soon a small square doorframe took shape. After a few tugs with the crowbar, Bodhi pried the small door open with a loud creak. A burst of cold, metallic-smelling air drifted up. Bodhi poked his head into the darkness. "There's stairs."

Raven stepped back. "I can't. That's way too small for me. I lied when I said I was fearless. I get claustrophobic."

"You brought a flashlight, right?" Devon asked.

"What do you think? Come on, this is what we're here for." Bodhi lowered himself through the door, his backpack hitting the edges as he descended.

Raven nudged Devon. "I'll keep an eye out. You got this."

Bodhi was right. She nodded, steeling herself, took a gulp of air, and stepped down. Instantly she could feel the cold from the stone steps sneak up her legs. Bodhi turned on his flashlight. A stone tunnel appeared, arching overhead. Bodhi reached the bottom. His flashlight beam bounced and disappeared around a corner.

Devon landed on the flat ground and turned the corner to find Bodhi staring at a wall full of shelves. A few small wooden crates and one metal box were all that was left. "Let's get this stuff outside," Bodhi whispered, panting.

He set his flashlight on a shelf and handed Devon the metal box. She took it with her free hand. It was lighter than she expected.

Bodhi pulled out a crate filled with mason jars, each stuffed with what looked like dirt. He caught her puzzled stare. "Someone thought it was important enough to store and save, so I'm bringing it out with us," he said.

"Good idea." Clinging to her flashlight, Devon tucked the box against her body. She shivered. "I'm freezing. Raven? You out there?" She started to climb back out and held the box through the small door overhead, but Raven didn't respond. Devon hoisted herself up and outside again. "Rav?" she yelled in the direction of the car.

"Up here!" Raven called back.

"We found something! Come down!" Devon used the crowbar to pry open the metal box. Inside was a single manila envelope sealed with a faded red string. Devon untied it and pulled out a sheet of paper.

*We, the undersigned, agree to the following terms of
ownership:*
*The purchase of Lot #1882-A from United States
Department of Defense-*
　　　　　Francis Keaton: 50%
　　　　　Reed Hutchins: 25%
　　　　　Edward Dover: 25%
*All parties agree that any future sale of a portion of
this Lot must be agreed to by ALL descendants.*

Devon reread the document. Keaton, Hutchins, and Dover had
all agreed on how the land was to be treated. This document probably had some historical significance as far as The Keaton School
went . . . but it wasn't exactly buried treasure. This couldn't be why
Reed wanted her to find, could it?

Bodhi emerged from the underground room, pushing the jar-
filled crate out ahead of him. "What did you get?"

"I think it's an early deed to the land or something."

"Let's bring it up to the house. Where's Raven?"

"Up top," Devon said. She was careful not to bend the dry paper
as she put it back in the envelope.

"Rave?" Bodhi yelled. There was no response. The metal cable
started to quiver next to them. Devon and Bodhi traded a confused
look.

"Raven?" Devon yelled. The cable swayed more, followed by
the sound of the car starting up. "What the—"

Raven screamed.

Bodhi pushed Devon against the cement wall, his hands tight
around her arms. "Stay here!"

He turned to run to Raven, but the metal cable must have been
cut from above, because it was suddenly hurling toward them. He
ducked as the cable lashed at the ground, breaking a few branches
along the way before hanging like a renegade question mark. But

he didn't hesitate. He jumped up, grabbed the ledge, and pulled himself over it, vanishing overhead.

Devon could only hear her own fast breathing. She looked down and saw that her hands were pressed into the groove of Reed's palms. It was the only comfort she had. Raven must have fallen; maybe she tried to move the car? The terror rising up the back of her throat told Devon that was wishful thinking. She immediately thought of the photos of her and Raven at the deli. Had their stalker come up to campus? Why hadn't she told Raven? It had been a stupid move.

She quickly tucked Reed's envelope into her jeans and under her jacket against her back.

Better to leave the metal box down here in case there was trouble.

"Dev! Come up!" Bodhi yelled.

His voice sounded urgent but not panicked. Whatever danger there was had now passed, Devon reasoned. She hoisted herself over the ledge as he'd done, crawling in the dirt at the steepest parts. Finally she broke into a run.

Bodhi was helping Raven into the backseat of the car. Devon caught a glimpse of blood on her leg, and her shoe was matted with dirt. "We gotta go. Get in." Devon ran to the passenger side and started to get in when she glimpsed a shadow on the grassy slope above, in the direction of campus.

"Devon Mackintosh, that you?"

The mysterious figure didn't sound like a student, more like a concerned teacher. The glare of the sun made him impossible to identify. *Damn, now Keaton knows we're down here.* Not that it mattered anymore. All that mattered was getting Raven help.

CHAPTER 19

Raven's foot and ankle were broken, but she wouldn't need surgery. Bodhi didn't want to leave her side at the hospital, though Raven insisted she was too high on painkillers to miss him if he took Devon back to school. And it was late. Devon didn't want to appear antsy, but eight straight hours in the E.R. was beginning to take its toll. And she couldn't be late for curfew, not with the campus buzzing with who-knows-what.

The hidden paper poked into her shoulder blades. She was too nervous about who might be watching to move them. Even worse, Raven couldn't remember much about what happened, which only made Devon more paranoid.

According to Raven, she'd spotted a guy starting their car. Raven apparently opened the driver's door and tried to pull him out, and the front tire ended up rolling over her foot. The guy ran toward the Keaton campus, and Raven couldn't remember what he looked like, other than that he was wearing a Keaton baseball hat. A new baseball hat—that much she remembered. Devon had to ask, but Raven said she didn't notice any dimples in his cheeks. Then again, the guy probably wasn't smiling.

Maybe it wasn't Eli. Maybe it was Khaki.

"What do you think, Dev?" Bodhi said. "I should probably get you home."

Raven was staring glassy-eyed at an infomercial for a "revolutionary" vegetable-cutting set. Machines hummed and beeped around her.

Devon nodded, resisting the urge to crawl into the hospital bed and hug Raven. "I'm going to check around the hillside. Maybe he dropped something when he ran away." She fought the fear of being watched, the idea that Raven's nurse was listening to their conversations, that cameras were snapping their every move. There would be clues left on the hillside, and she would find them. But today's incident had planted a darker idea in her mind: they weren't safe on campus, after all.

The Hutchins family had used Grant to get to her last semester; it couldn't be that difficult to put a new student on the payroll. An image of Oz flashed in her head. He was new and conveniently very close to Cleo. And Cleo was conveniently close to Devon. Not to mention, he'd already tried to hide one thing. Maybe he was hiding lots more.

BODHI'S HAND WAS POISED over the key in the ignition, but he couldn't seem to start the car. Instead he just stared at the steering wheel, sitting in silence in the hospital parking lot. Devon reached over and rubbed the back of his neck. Bodhi bowed his head. Even though she couldn't see the tears, she knew he was crying.

"It's not always going to be like this," Devon soothed. "I don't know why all this is happening, but we're going to solve it."

He sniffed and shook his head, straightening up. "If something had happened to her, I don't think I could have handled it." His voice was thick. "I'm supposed to protect her. I'm supposed to make sure she *doesn't* end up in the hospital."

Devon leaned over the console and pulled Bodhi's face to hers. She kissed his lips, wet with tears. He pulled her closer and kissed her back.

Her cell phone rang. She pulled away and fumbled for it. *Mom. Uh-oh.* Bodhi cleared his throat, rubbed his eyes, and started the car while Devon answered.

"Devon? Where are you?" Her mom sounded frantic.

"Headed back to school." Devon and Bodhi exchanged a look. "Oh, no, they called you, didn't they?"

"Someone saw you leave campus with that Elliot boy. They weren't sure if you were hurt. They asked me if they should call the police. Devon, you're okay, aren't you?"

"I'm fine, Mom. I'll be back at school in twenty minutes. Who called you—"

"I'm on my way, too."

"What? No, you don't have to do that."

"Devon, they asked me to." Her mom hung up.

"What'd she say?" Bodhi asked. His eyes stayed on the road.

"I'm screwed," Devon said, feeling sick. "Really screwed."

CHAPTER 20

Disciplinary committees were rarely convened at Keaton, and only in true emergencies. There had been only one last year, when Kevin Cosmo had showed up to formal dinner blatantly drunk. Devon vividly remembered the silence that had fallen over the whole hillside during the hour-long proceeding, as if everyone was waiting to hear the results broadcast across campus.

Kevin Cosmo had gotten kicked out.

Now, sitting at the large table in the faculty conference room, she realized that it might be her turn. No doubt she'd been the focal point of whispered gossip over dinner. Just knowing that made her cheeks burn and her palms sweat. But of course she could live with that. Who was she kidding? It was the row of grim faces—including Headmaster Wyler and Dr. Hsu—staring her down that was too much.

Headmaster Wyler was still working his way through the litany of Devon's wrongdoings. He'd been prattling on for over ten minutes.

"Bodhi Elliot had been explicitly banned from the Keaton campus. And yet you consort with him on grounds where you are forbidden to go. All this after your continued reticence to adhere to the Keaton rulebook. Frankly, I'm disappointed in you, Devon. I thought we were working together." Headmaster Wyler pressed his palms flat on the table and nodded at Devon. She didn't know if she was supposed to say anything, but she knew it was too late for excuses.

"Now, I think given your past probationary status in addition to today's incident, a two-week suspension seems appropriate."

The edges of Devon's vision started to go fuzzy, like a dark room closing in on all sides. She hoped she wouldn't faint right here.

He cleared his throat. "We also received a call this week about your scholarship. It seems that your benefactor has had to withdraw your funding. These two incidents are unrelated, but we are inclined to send you home for the suspension, during which time we'll try to find other means to reinstate your financial assistance for your return. But keep in mind that, given your current record, it might be harder than we originally anticipated. Do you understand what I'm telling you?"

Devon's eyes burned into his. "My scholarship was pulled? By who? I mean, whom? Don't I have a right to know?" She turned to Dr. Hsu, who looked sheepish. "So, okay. I'm suspended, fine. I get that. I know what I did wrong. No one seems interested in *why* I was down at the Palace, but whatever, you probably wouldn't believe me, anyways. But I'm just supposed to go home and hope what? That somebody somewhere magically steps in to pay for the rest of my semester?"

The blackness around Devon's vision had turned into white, searing light. Fear transformed to fury. While the school was clinging to its rulebook, her whole life was getting rearranged, and no one seemed to care.

Headmaster Wyler straightened his papers. Then other faculty members began to leave as well. Only Dr. Hsu remained still. "Your mom will be waiting for you in your dorm," Headmaster Wyler concluded. "We think it's best if you leave tonight. And Devon, we want you back here, but only in the best circumstances for everyone." He gave her a begrudging close-mouthed smile. Devon had seen that smile enough to know it was purely for show.

"So that's it? I'm done?" Devon stood up before they could answer. Dr. Hsu remained in her seat, her eyes fixed on the tabletop. "Thanks for keeping our sessions confidential, Doc."

With that, she stormed out and started running. She kept to the shadows. The light rain felt good on her burning cheeks. Her mom's car was in the parking lot below Bay House, and the light was on inside her room. No doubt her mom had packed a bag for her already, probably with Presley's help. Poor Presley. Devon had ruined her spring break college tour.

She stepped on the gravel pathway leading around to the side entrance of Bay House. The crunch of the gravel against the silence of campus made her stop. Whoever had assaulted Raven at the Palace had probably come back through campus this way. Maybe there was . . .

Devon sighed; what was she doing? She was hardly going to start looking for footprints moments after getting kicked out of Keaton. *Stop it, Devon. You have to stop obsessing.*

She turned her face up to the night sky and let the drizzle land on her face, her hair, and her jacket as if it could cool her simmering thoughts. With one last deep breath, Devon steeled herself to face her mom. She reached for the door, and that's when she spotted the Keaton baseball hat perfectly perched on the hedge next to her dorm doorway.

CHAPTER 21

When she woke up in her own bed in her own house the next morning, Devon had to remind herself what had happened at school last night. She hoped she could put off facing the reality of today for at least another hour. Maybe if she was quiet in bed, her mom wouldn't bug her. She dug Reed's diary out from her backpack.

September 22, 1942

Athena has been crying all day. I can't fault her for that. The screaming woke us up first. Then Dr. Keaton, yelling Hana's name. By the time Athena and I were outside, all we saw was the lights from the Army jeeps disappearing down the hill. Keaton wailed in his cabin. It's the only way I can properly describe it. Wailed like an animal. Athena made him tea to calm him down even though I could see her hands shaking as she poured it.

It happened. They changed their minds. The Army decided that having a Japanese-American in our camp, despite the fact that Hana was born in Oakland, was too dangerous. So they took her. They must have known it was wrong, because why else would they do it in the middle of the night?

Dr. Keaton has spent the last few days trying to find where she was sent, trying to send at least a suitcase full of clothes to her. Dr. Keaton is scared they might treat her like a spy. Interrogate her like a spy. Athena and I pray every night for Hana's safe and quick return. The atrocities of this war aren't just happening overseas.

Devon couldn't read anymore. Apparently things were crappy in the past, too. Keaton's wife was just taken in the middle of the night like that? No trial, no arrest, no warning, even? It was hard to believe that all happened on the Keaton hillside while Reed had lived there.

Downstairs she heard the front door close, followed by her mom's car starting. *Time to get up and figure out the rest of your life*, she thought.

First and foremost, would she have a life? How the hell would she get this stalker situation under control? Eli on the boat, the stranger in Berkeley, and now someone at Keaton—they all had to come from the same source. And it would be safe to assume that this source knew that Devon was back in Berkeley now.

She eyed the Keaton baseball hat she had shoved into her backpack last night. A guy wearing this hat—that's all she had to go on to help Raven. Even inspecting the inside lining yielded no helpful results. A single strand of hair would have been helpful, but Devon was no C.S.I. expert. Now that she wasn't on campus, her ability to check on Oz's alibi was limited. And asking Cleo invasive questions probably wouldn't be appreciated.

Who knew what Cleo even thought of her anymore? Maybe Devon had been relegated to the past, disappeared like Hana, another Keaton tragedy that would be swept away and forgotten.

What happened when people started over at a new school mid-year?

Actually, that was a good thought. She knew someone who'd started over: Oz.

St. Matthews had a similar kind of reputation and vibe as The Keaton School, the same wealth and connections. Except here in the city, the students wore stiff uniforms and went home every night. They also prayed in chapel, apparently.

Devon waited outside the school gates as the final bell rang at three o'clock. The campus was more compact and homogeneous than Keaton: clean white Spanish stucco, red tiled roofs, the parking lot packed with gleaming high-end cars. *Ah, another day for San Francisco's elite.* Devon tried to quell her resentment and focus.

She didn't know exactly who she was looking for, but she knew Cleo had old friends here, friends who probably knew Oz as well. If she could find the most fashion-conscious junior in the group of uniforms, she might get lucky . . .

Younger kids, freshmen, were the first to hurry past. The older kids were walking slower, talking in groups as they went. Most gave her a quick once-over, the interloper in their tightly knit system.

Maybe it was time for Plan B. Devon put the Keaton baseball cap on her head. The once-overs turned to slight smiles from a few passing students. One girl, tall and painfully skinny with peroxide-blonde hair, stopped and raised an eyebrow. "You go to Keaton? I know some kids there."

"Oh, cool. I was hoping to run into someone—"

"Slow down, Chatty Cathy." The girl tossed her chin in the direction of the parking lot. "Lemme get off campus first. I need a cigarette. Fucking mid-terms."

Devon bit her tongue and followed the girl to the parking lot. The girl's hands shook slightly as she unlocked her cherry-red Prius. She sat in the driver's seat, door still open, and lit a smoke from her glove compartment.

"This is considered off campus?" Devon asked nervously.

The girl smirked. She exhaled out of the corner of her mouth, away from Devon. "Close enough. Who you looking for? I'm Mattie, by the way." She extended a hand, now steady. "Sorry if I was rude before. Jonesing."

Devon offered a forgiving smile. "No worries. You don't know Cleo Lambert by any chance, do you?"

Mattie exhaled quickly, her face lighting up. "Hell, yes! We went to middle school together before I came to this shit-hole. You friends with her at Keaton?"

"Yeah, except . . . Well, when was the last time you spoke to her?"

Mattie shrugged. "Don't know. We texted a month or so back. Reminded me you guys got Oz." She wriggled her eyebrows. "How's that working out?"

"Good. I mean, he's cool. Fits in well." Devon struggled to find the right answer without knowing anything about Mattie.

"Bullshit. The girls are fighting over him, aren't they?"

Devon had to laugh. "Well, yeah, that's part of it."

"I figured he'd play it that way." She ashed on the pavement and shook her head. "Front like he's single."

"Isn't he?"

Mattie pointed across the parking lot at a blonde with long hair in a fishtail braid. The girl was laughing with a few other blondes in volleyball uniforms. "Might want to ask Nikki. She seems to think they're still together. Apparently he calls her every night. They're like, *in love*, or something like that."

The same words Cleo used. "That's, um, illuminating." Devon said. Her throat tightened.

"Illuminating? Okay, Miss Keaton Vocab." Mattie grinned. "Just playing. I gotta get going. Tell Cleo I miss that slut." She stomped out her cigarette.

"I will. Thanks for the chat."

"What's this all about, anyway?" Mattie was already starting her car. "You scoping out your new school? You get kicked out or something?"

Devon sighed. "Honestly, I don't know."

Mattie's smile softened. "If you want to get in trouble here, you know where to find me." She gave Devon a short wave and peeled out of the parking lot.

Devon watched her go, remembering Oz's dopey, flustered face when he'd lied about Nikki's text in Cleo's car. He wasn't another Grant. Besides, he'd agreed to do Cleo the favor of spying on C.C. Tran, even though it clearly annoyed his older sister. The evidence pointed one way: he was trying to ingratiate himself with Cleo by being Mr. Nice Guy with her troubled friend Devon—overcompensating while trying to hide his cheating. He had no idea what going on in Devon's life, really.

Besides, he didn't seem that bright.

So for now she could cross him off her list. It was an assumption, but one she was willing to make. And at the very least, she could give Cleo a heads-up. She headed for Broadway, hoping to catch a bus that didn't pass right by Huntington House. The likelihood that she'd run into Eli was small, but she didn't want to stir up unnecessary attention. As far she knew, whoever was stalking her on campus didn't know she had left Keaton.

Her phone vibrated in her pocket. *Ugh.* Probably Mom, wondering why she wasn't at home . . . No. A blocked number. "Hello?"

"Is it nice to be back in the city?" a boy's voice on the other end asked.

Devon froze. "Eric?"

"I heard you got into a little trouble. Seems out of character for you."

"How did you know? Eric, what the hell is—"

"My attorney called this morning. Seems you won't be testifying at my trial any longer. Now that you're not a credible witness."

Devon stood in the middle of the sidewalk, blood turning to ice in her veins. A bus whizzed past, kicking up leaves and dirt. She turned around, feeling exposed, vulnerable, a target. *Eric Hutchins.* She'd been wrong to consider him even remotely human. Someone was probably stalking her right now on his behalf.

"But that's okay, because you're going to help me," Eric continued. "Maya needs to be there. The trial is next week. She's going to call you and tell you where she is. And I need you to go get her. If you do that, all your problems will go away. Everyone wins."

"What the hell are you talking about?" Devon demanded. "This is twisted. Why would I help you? Let's start there before you blackmail me." She ducked into an alcove in front of a closed restaurant to hear above the roar of traffic.

"Where are you?" Eric asked. "You're suspended. Shouldn't you be at home?"

"What the hell do you care?" she snapped.

"You want to go back to Keaton, right? I can make that happen for you."

"You? So it *is* your family that pays my scholarship—"

"Wrong again, Mackintosh. We never paid for your scholarship, but I can arrange for a new one, courtesy of the Hutchins family. And then you'll be fine."

Devon kept scanning the street. "Why me? If you guys need Maya so badly, why won't your parents go? Or hers?"

Eric didn't answer.

"Hello?"

"Our parents don't really know." The shift in his tone was abrupt. No more smarminess; it was almost pleading. "She needs to be at the trial. Devon, if I go to jail, this will be my last chance to see her. I need her here. You have to help us."

There was shaky emotion underneath the arrogance. Not that Devon felt anything, or even pitied him. He was probably doomed to a life in prison—an imprisonment he deserved—whether Devon testified or not. It was a desperate move on his part. On the other hand, she'd been suspended. She had two weeks to kill with her mom at work the whole time. And if this could help her find out who *did* pay for her scholarship, then she might find out who had sent Eli and Khaki, maybe even why Reed had been so obsessed with giving her that diary . . .

She had a sudden queasy feeling Eric knew the answers to all these questions. There was a reason he'd called her now. Today. Even if he wasn't watching. He needed to someone to do his dirty work, and Devon fit the bill.

"Maya's going to call you soon," Eric said. "She'll tell you how to get a car."

Devon swallowed. "I didn't say I'd do it." But the words were weak, barely a whisper. She didn't have a choice, did she?

"I'm sure you'll get over that," Eric said, as if reading her mind.

There was a click, and the line went dead.

CHAPTER 22

At first, Devon wondered if she were hallucinating. That couldn't be Bodhi sitting on her front step. The person she wanted to see most couldn't be waiting for her after the most nerve-wracking bus ride of her life. Better still, her mom's car wasn't in the driveway. She was still at work, even though she'd promised to be home by four o'clock. It was already four fifteen, so there would be no awkward introduction.

"How did you know where I live?" Devon asked, collapsing into his arms as he stood to greet her. "Oh, right," she murmured, closing her eyes as she nuzzled against his poncho, breathing in the familiar coconut smell. Amazing how one whiff of that could calm her down. "You have magic powers."

"If you call a Wi-Fi connection and a little HTML know-how magic, then yeah." He chuckled, then drew in a sharp breath. "I'm so sorry. I couldn't stay away. I'm sure I just made it worse for you—"

Devon cut him off by kissing him. She pulled back. "You make everything better for me. Screw them if they think otherwise."

He tucked her hair behind her ears and looked into her eyes. "Maybe it's better, safer, if you're here for now."

Devon almost laughed. The word "safe" had lost all meaning. "How's Raven?" she asked, anxious again. "I mean, where is she?"

"Still at the hospital, but good. I'm taking her home tonight when I get back. I just needed to see you when I heard that Keaton kicked you to the curb."

"How did you hear, by the way?" Devon asked, sitting down on the steps. "Because word has spread quicker than most Keaton news."

"Cleo called me. Thought I'd want to know."

"Eric called *me*," Devon responded.

Bodhi tilted his head. "What?"

"It gets worse. I have to do him a favor. I'm going to Montana to get Maya out of her pregnancy home, or whatever it's called."

Bodhi chewed his lip and sat beside her, his hand on her knee. "What could Eric Hutchins possibly have on you to make you do this? What's going on?"

Devon dug her nails into her palm. She didn't want to keep anything from Bodhi, but the truth was embarrassing to admit. "My scholarship got taken away. He says his family isn't paying it, but I can't think of why it would get defunded now. The timing isn't random, I'm sure. If the Hutchinses aren't paying it, Eric knows who is. And without it, I can't go back."

Bodhi's lips twisted in anger, his eyes smoldering. "There's going to be a time when they can't mess with us anymore. Reed gave everything to Raven and me for a reason—to stop them from screwing with people. You shouldn't have to do this."

"You . . . I know what you're saying." Devon's eyes welled with tears. "But I have to do this. I have to fall into this trap, because it's the only way I'll learn the truth. It's worth it. Let's just think of it as a keep-your-enemies-close kind of thing. Do Eric a favor, see what we find out, and maybe something good will come of it."

Bodhi pulled her into his chest, his chin resting on top of her head. "You're a hell of a lot braver than I am," he breathed.

"No, I'm not. Just more selfish."

He laughed. "I'm pretty selfish, too. So if you go . . . come back quickly."

Devon nuzzled her cold nose against his neck. "I have to ask one more favor. Can you help track the IP address from that email Isaac Green gave me? I think Raven sent an email out, but if they responded, it's all probably with her."

He kissed her. "Okay. That I can do. But only if you stay in touch the entire time you're on the road. Deal?"

"Deal." He stood, but she pulled him back and kissed him again, this time for a while. She didn't care if Mom interrupted. Now she truly had nothing to lose except Bodhi—and she knew that she couldn't, no matter what happened.

MOM STILL WASN'T HOME when dinnertime rolled around. Devon rummaged in the pantry, hoping for some macaroni and cheese or something equally processed yet comforting. SpaghettiOs would work.

She double-checked the sticky notes on the fridge. Her mother had left without a word this morning, naturally. The silent treatment was par for the course in this situation. But now Devon was worried. Her only child had been suspended, and she'd promised to be home three hours ago. It was unlike her not to be in contact all day. Could something at work be more pressing than this?

Devon finished her last slurp of soup and almost unconsciously wandered upstairs to her mom's room. But as she eyed the bedroom, she thought about that phone number she'd photographed.

The aged paperback was long gone; there were no books on her bed-side table. A few discarded blouses were on the bed, and there were the sneakers she had worn last night to pick Devon up at school, but nothing out of the ordinary. Devon flipped through her pictures in her phone to find the image with the number. It couldn't hurt to try it, could it? Maybe best to try it from the home phone instead of her cell; that way the recipient—if the number was even still in service, if the recipient even knew her mother—wouldn't be suspicious.

She dialed.

It rang, so at least it was still a working number. After a few rings, a man's voice picked up. "Forget something?" He sounded friendly but terse, like he was busy with something else. Devon didn't say anything.

"Karen?"

So this stranger clearly did know her mother. Devon didn't know whether she should announce herself or not. *Damn, damn, damn.* She should have thought this through. She hadn't actually expected anyone to pick up.

"Um . . ." was all she managed to stammer.

He immediately hung up.

Devon stood there, petrified, until she heard her mom's car pull into the driveway. Fighting to remain calm, she made sure she hadn't left anything undone in her mom's room and ran downstairs.

"Hi, honey! Sorry I'm late!"

Cheeriness. No probing questions about how Devon had spent her day or how Devon intended to atone for her terrible mistakes. No, her mom was armed with takeout Thai and blathering apolo-gies. Boring staff meetings had kept her at the office. Devon let her rant. For all Devon knew, Mom could have spent the day at Keaton pleading with the headmaster. Of all the people in her life who might be conspiring against her, Devon knew her mother wasn't among them. Which made the fact that Mom was lying right now all the more horrifying.

∞

AFTER A PAINFUL DINNER during which Mom suddenly remembered that she had to be a disciplinarian, Devon disappeared into
her bedroom. She saw that Cleo was online. Video chatting might
be too weird. Devon opted to send a text instead. Hi.

Cleo responded a minute later: Bonjour! How's the suspension?
Met Mattie today.

A longer pause this time.

Too much free time on your hands? ☺

Cleo might have been joking, but it was still a jab. Devon had to
tell Cleo what Mattie said. She would want to know the truth about
Bodhi if their roles were reversed. Even if it meant Cleo might hate
her for it. She had to.

Ask Oz about Nikki.

Cleo waited almost five minutes before replying. Dev, u srsly
have 2 stop.

And then she was gone.

CHAPTER 23

Maya called in the middle of the night. 2:38 A.M., specifically, because Devon stared at her phone for a few seconds, desperately hoping it was Cleo or Bodhi. The 406 area code made it clear that the caller wasn't either.

"Devon?" Maya whispered.

"I'm here," Devon said, now wide awake. "Eric said you'd be calling. He didn't mention it would be so late, though." She pulled the comforter over her head to keep the noise from reaching her mom down the hall.

"I don't have a phone up here. They took it. Listen, I'm sending a car service for you tomorrow at ten A.M. It will bring you here. You have an appointment set up under the name Chelsea Ford."

Devon's pulse quickened. "Am I supposed to be writing this down?"

"Chelsea Ford. That's all you need to remember. They'll pick you up tomorrow morning at ten A.M. I gotta go." Maya hung up.

Devon checked the time on her phone. 2:39 A.M. It had happened so quickly, she needed to remind herself that she wasn't dreaming. If it was a dream, Maya might have said *thank you.* But gratitude had never been Maya's style.

A BLACK SUV APPEARED across the street as Devon waited by the window. She looked at her phone with bleary eyes: 10:03.

A driver in a uniform unfolded a paper in the front seat. He caught Devon peering at him and nodded at her. Devon ducked back inside and played out the worst-case scenario in her mind: what if Maya and Eric had paid this driver to make her disappear? She didn't know this driver or the company he was with—too many unknowns for her liking. The one thing she knew was that Eric's desire to see Maya before his trial was real, because the crime of murdering his brother was real. He was guilty; it was just a matter of sentencing. Ergo, if she wanted to learn the truth and possibly save her life at Keaton, she had no other option.

Devon had made up a thin excuse about spending the night with Ariel, her old friend from home. Basically, if she didn't return to Keaton, she needed to reconnect with public school in a hurry. Her mom praised her for her "mature thinking." She'd even used those exact words, words she would normally never use. Her mom was hiding something, too, so what the hell? They could hide together by being apart.

Before she locked up, she made another attempt at dialing the mysterious number from the paperback.

It was disconnected.

TWENTY-ONE HOURS LATER, DEVON woke up at dawn in the backseat of the SUV as the driver pulled over at a gas station. The temperatures were lower; snow stuck to the metal lampposts on every corner like a bumpy layer of spray paint. Beyond the short block of stores nearby, Devon could see miles of white prairie, tinged pink in the sunlight, leading to snow-capped mountains ahead. Good thing she'd grabbed a heavy jacket and hat from her coat rack at the last second.

"Where are we?" she croaked groggily.

"Bozeman," the driver replied in the rearview mirror. "St. Mary's is just on the other end of town."

"I think I fell asleep somewhere in Nevada," Devon said, yawning. "Wait, how are you still awake?"

The driver smiled. "I pulled over and slept for a few hours. I don't need much sleep. Part of the job." He popped the door on the gas tank and hopped out of the car.

Stretching her legs sounded good. Devon flung open the door and jumped out also. "Okay if I use the bathroom?" she asked.

"It's your dollar, ma'am," he replied politely and flipped the switch on the gas pump.

Right. This isn't technically a kidnapping. "I'm going to grab something inside, too. Want anything?"

"I'm fine, thanks."

The gas station store was like any other, although Devon noticed the vast varieties of jerky. Deer jerky. Bison jerky. Elk jerky. Moose jerky. *Could they really taste that different?* The pimply guy behind the counter looked to be in his late teens, early twenties. Devon wondered how much the local town knew about St. Mary's. Any hints about what she was walking into might come in handy. "I'm visiting a friend at St. Mary's. Have you heard of it by any chance?"

He snickered. "The one with all the pregnant girls? I've never seen the girls here. Apparently the nuns don't want them talking to any of the men in town."

"Oh, yeah?" Devon prodded.

"My buddy tried to sneak a girl out of there, and some nun drove him off the hill with a shotgun. They're not messing around up there. That I know." He ran his hand along the rim of his frayed baseball cap and eyed the black Escalade. "Good luck, miss," he whispered as he rang up her bottle of water.

He probably thought she was pregnant, Devon realized as she got back in the car. She was glad she'd asked. A nun with a shotgun was an image Devon couldn't shake. Maya had conveniently left that part out.

Before she returned to the car, Devon texted Bodhi. I'm okay. More soon.

The wrought-iron gate was flanked by two stone walls. A small oval-shaped sign hung on the left wall: *St. Mary's School for Girls.* A video camera was mounted at the top of the wall, positioned perfectly to observe any incoming cars.

The intercom next to the driveway squealed to life as a woman's voice asked, "Do you have an appointment?"

The driver looked at Devon in the rearview mirror. "Do we?"

"Yes, tell her Chelsea Ford is here."

The driver rolled down his window. "Yes, I'm delivering Miss Ford for her appointment with you. Chelsea Ford."

The intercom clicked off. They waited in silence as the wind whistled around them. Devon noticed the driver stealing glances at her in the backseat.

"What's your name? I'm sorry I didn't ask," Devon said.

"Kevin," he said. "I know you're no Chelsea Ford, but that's fine. The less I know, the better." He flashed a toothy grin.

Devon smiled, relieved she didn't have to try to lie to the guy who probably heard her snoring while he drove. "That's probably a good idea."

With a screeching dial tone, the gates slowly swung open.

"So far, so good," Kevin said. He shifted gears, and the SUV climbed up the driveway. The house at the top of the hill wasn't what Devon expected. It was sleek and modern and huge, with vast wood-paneled wings. She thought it would look like a nineteenth-century Colonial with a wraparound porch. In her mind, this place, even just the idea of it, was a relic from another era. But apparently in the current era, the underage pregnancy business paid pretty well.

A nun dressed in full regalia was already walking toward their car as they pulled in. Her cheeks were pink in the cold Montana air, and her breath was visible in the dawn light. She was surprisingly young.

Kevin walked around and opened Devon's door for her.

"You must be Chelsea," the nun said, extending a hand to Devon. She scanned Devon up and down. Probably guessing if she was pregnant or not, Devon thought. Maya never said anything about Chelsea Ford being pregnant.

"Thanks for having me," Devon said.

"I'm Sister Louise. Let's get out of this cold, shall we?" The nun smiled, but Devon could see her jaw was clenched. The gas station attendant was right; visitors were probably not welcome around here. Sister Louise showed Devon to the front door, complete with a horseshoe for a handle. Devon turned around and saw Kevin leaning against the car, blowing into his hands against the cold air. He nodded. Next time she got in that car, Maya would be with her, and they'd probably be running.

Inside looked more like a spa than a boarding school. The walls were painted a warm yellow color. A pitcher of water sat on its own small table with a handwritten sign that read: *Stay hydrated!* The whole room had turquoise accents and lots of Native American art and blankets.

A girl who couldn't be more than fifteen sat behind a desk, one hand resting on her pregnant stomach. She wore an oversized men's plaid flannel shirt with leggings and furry boots and had pulled her hair into a messy bun.

"Hi, I'm Reina," she said with a bright smile and extended a hand to Devon.

"Chelsea," Devon replied.

"Reina is one of our newer arrivals. She's been on front desk duty this week. Let me give you a tour, and then we can talk a little more personally, hmm?" Sister Louise offered a knowing smile. Reina gave Devon the same. *Yep, they all think I'm pregnant. Thanks, Maya.* "Let's start with the study rooms."

She led Devon down a long hall lined with six private study rooms, all with large glass doors and a lone pregnant teenager studying inside. The girls eyed Devon, each one glancing at her flat stomach, before a look from Sister Louise sent them back to their books. Privacy was probably rare at a place like this. She kept hoping Maya would be in the next study room or suddenly come around the corner.

Did Maya even know she was here? What exactly was her plan at this point?

At the end of the hall was a larger room with a kitchen setup on one side and a nursery on the other. "This is our practical education lab. We try to help the girls learn to cook for themselves and learn about proper food and nutrition for their growing babies."

Devon nodded politely.

They passed the front desk again, where Reina smiled at Devon but went back to her homework. The next hallway wing had rows of closed doors, none of which were glass. These rooms were private; maybe Maya was in one of them. Devon reached for a door handle.

"Could I use the bathroom?" she asked.

"Yes, but that's not the bathroom," Sister Louise snapped.

Devon already had the door open. Inside, an older nun sat at a desk, her head bent in prayer. Across from the desk, facing the wall, was a girl kneeling on a small stool, head bent in prayer as well. The older nun looked up, her face dry and cracked with wrinkles and frown lines. The girl stayed kneeling but looked up, too.

Maya. Devon blinked.

They locked eyes, and Maya quickly put her head back down. Devon could hear her whispering a *Hail Mary*.

"This is a restricted area," the old nun said. She stood and approached Devon. Tall, with football player-sized shoulders, the nun filled the doorframe, forcing Devon back into the hallway.

"I'm sorry, Sister Helen," Sister Louise muttered. "She was faster than me."

Devon noticed a glass case behind the nun's desk, multiple rifles standing at attention inside. Across the room, Maya hadn't moved. What was she waiting for? Sister Helen closed the door, its lock clicking into place.

"Why don't we head to my office for our chat?" Sister Louise offered.

Devon did not want to get stuck in this nun's office while struggling to hold up her thin lies. "That sounds like a great idea. But if you'll give me a minute, I really need to use the bathroom—"

A scream came from Sister Helen's room, cutting her off.

The door slammed open against the wall. Maya lurched into the hall, clutching her stomach with an agonized look on her face. "The baby's coming," she gasped between short breaths. "I have to go now. Call an ambulance."

"Call the ambulance," Sister Helen yelled back at Reina. "Tell them we have a baby coming." Reina called 911 from the phone on her desk.

Sister Helen tried to steer Maya away from the door, but Maya went limp in her arms. "You'll be fine, Maya. This is just a contraction. You probably have a few hours until the baby comes. Breathe like we talked about . . ."

"Please, it hurts," Maya moaned. "Something's not right. Let me go to the hospital. The ambulance won't get here in time."

Devon pounced on her cue. "I have a car here. We could take her."

Sister Helen's grip on Maya's arm tightened. "I'm sorry, we're not supposed to let these girls out of our sight. They are under our guardianship."

"Then you can ride with us," Devon answered. "You don't have to leave her, but we can honestly get her there faster than waiting for the ambulance."

"Just—just get me to the hospital," Maya stammered. She waddled to the front door, pulling the nun along with her, straight toward the SUV. Kevin quickly ran around to open the back door for her. Devon helped hoist Maya into the seat.

"Sister Louise, you go with Maya. Call me when you get there," Sister Helen commanded. Sister Louise nodded vigorously; she almost seemed excited about going to the hospital. Devon ran around front and hopped into the passenger seat. Doors slammed, Kevin revved the engine, and they were barreling down the driveway.

Devon had to hand it to Maya: the girl could act. She kept up the panting and crying the entire forty-five minutes it took to reach the hospital as Sister Louise rubbed Maya's hand and coached her breathing. When they pulled up to the hospital entrance, Sister Louise instructed Devon to get a wheelchair to help Maya get inside.

"No," Maya interjected. "Get them to find Dr. Collins. See if he's here."

Sister Louise nodded. "Right, right. Dr. Collins. Wait for me here; I'll be back with a nurse." She jumped out of the SUV and ran into the emergency room, her long black skirt flapping behind her in the wind.

"Get the hell out of here!" Maya barked at Kevin. She reached over and pulled the backseat door closed. "Now! Get to the highway and go west!"

Kevin needed no further instruction. He screeched into reverse, spun around, and sped toward the highway.

Devon couldn't shake the image of the lone nun running into the hospital. "I can't believe that just happened," she said, gripping the door handle as the car swerved along the snowy roads.

"Thank God it did," Maya said. "Not that I've gone all religious or anything."

Devon stared at her. "But you're okay? No baby problems or anything?"

"Yeah, yeah, that was all a show." Maya started unraveling her braid. "We've had to watch all these birthing videos, so I've got the scream down. Plus, Sister Louise totally has a crush on Dr. Collins. She can't function around him; it's hilarious. She'll take way too long to put together what just happened, but when she does, Sister Helen is probably going to have her ass. Whatever. Probably wasn't going to be a good nun, anyways."

Devon couldn't believe how calm she was. "How soon do you think until they send out a search party? There's no way that older nun is going to take this lightly."

"We'll be fine. We can call off the search party when I show up back in San Francisco." Maya leaned her head back in her seat and closed her eyes, her hands resting across her stomach.

"Yeah, okay. It'll be fine," Devon said. If only she believed it.

You're welcome, she added.

CHAPTER 24

January 29, 1945

Our fears have come true, and it's worse than we ever thought possible. The war in Europe is almost over; the Allies are advancing on Germany now. And just a few weeks ago, we heard that the Japanese internment camps have started releasing people. Keaton has spent every morning watching the road up the hill, hoping for the cloud of dust that would bring Hana back home with it. Surely if people were being released, she would be returning as soon as she could.

Yesterday as we were eating dinner in the mess tent, we saw the cloud of dust down the hill. A car had dropped someone off near the bottom. A woman in a black dress carrying a small suitcase was walking up the hill alone. We all froze, and Keaton ran down the hill to greet her. But we knew something was wrong when Keaton stopped running before he reached the woman. "It's not her," Edward said behind me, his napkin still tucked into his shirt collar.

"Maybe it's her sister or a friend. She has news, whoever she is.

"But what are the odds it's good news?" Edward asked. He went back inside the mess tent to finish his dinner.

I ran to fetch Athena from our tent. "It's Hana. There's news," I told her. She was with the baby, and I remember her waiting, looking at me expectantly for the next sentence. But I didn't know what else to say. "Just come and see."

We hurried to the top of the road just as Keaton and the woman were arriving. Keaton was holding her suitcase and ushering her toward the mess tent. "Come, have some water. We have food, too. Anything you need."

Athena and I were speechless. For all we've seen of the newsreels of this war's atrocities, we have been spared much of its real misery. But this woman, her black hair was matted with dirt. Her skin hung over her cheekbones, limp and pale, and her eyes—I heard Athena inhale, and I knew she saw what I did in the woman's eyes. They were dark brown, almost black, and when she looked at us as she passed, it was as if she didn't even see us. As if she was still watching something else happen before her eyes, something she couldn't stop seeing.

We followed Keaton and the woman into the tent. She ate the rice and fish quickly, keeping her eyes glued to the plate. When her plate was empty, she took a long drink of her water before finally looking up at us. She gave Keaton a slight smile.

"Hana told me you would be nice to me," the woman said. "My name is Issa. We shared a tent in our camp. They took us to Wyoming. I was lucky and got on the first train leaving. But Hana, she asked that I find you."

Keaton reached across the table and took Issa's hand in his. "Please tell me where I can find her. I will go anywhere. Just tell me where."

She pulled her hand out of his and sighed. "Hana is still in Wyoming. We buried her there with your son."

Keaton couldn't hold the tears back any longer. "Son?" he choked out.

"Francis Ichiro Keaton," she told him. "Hana didn't know that she was pregnant when they took her. She was first sent to a detention center in Montana because of her marriage to you. They were convinced she was selling secrets to the Japanese, but Hana only swore her loyalty to America. By the time they sent her to Heart Mountain, she was six months pregnant and not doing well. I remember her skin almost looked gray when she arrived in our tent. I took care of her; we all tried. We gave her whatever we could of our own food, our clothes. She had gotten sick in the winter. Most of us didn't have warm enough clothes. She was starting to get healthier as it got warmer. She talked a lot about you, how proud she was of you and the work you were doing for the country. Despite everything they did to her, she still loved America. She talked about after the war, about the beautiful hillside you lived on and how she wanted to live there and raise your son. She named him Francis after you. Ichiro means 'first son' in Japanese. She wanted to have many children with you."

Keaton's head hung low, the tears dripping from his chin onto his khaki pants. Next to me on the bench, Athena cried while holding William. I kept looking at Issa. Was it possible any of this was false? Could Hana have gotten mixed up with someone else? It didn't seem true.

"He was born on May 6th, 1943. We had a nurse in our block that helped Hana, but there were complications. We didn't have a doctor, and we couldn't stop the bleeding. Francis lived for another day, but he was so small. I kept him with her until her body went cold. We tried to feed him goat's milk and water, but he followed his mother. He wouldn't have survived there another two years. This way they are together. We couldn't send a message to you because it was illegal to contact anyone in the military. We couldn't risk being sent to a more hostile detention center."

Issa reached into her jacket pocket and pulled out a small folded piece of paper. Inside was a gold ring. I recognized it as the same gold wedding band that Keaton wore. She gave it to Keaton. "This was hers. I'm sorry for the loss of your family, Mr. Keaton."

None of us knew what to say. The war had come home.

∞

DEVON MADE SURE MAYA had fallen asleep before she pulled out the fragile diary and finished the last of its worn pages. Maya needed frequent bathroom stops, and Devon tried to be supportive. But it was all about management of the pregnant girl. There wasn't a hint of what Devon would get in return for her service. *Maybe Maya doesn't know,* Devon thought, and texted Bodhi as much.

Mom didn't put up a fight when Devon had texted that she'd be spending another night at Ariel's. Apparently it was a "busy time" at the hospital.

Lies upon lies upon lies . . .

She tried to stay awake as they drove through Montana and Nevada, but nodded off after a huge silent meal the three of them shared at a rest stop before they reached the California border sometime in the middle of the night.

Devon woke up around dawn when the car jerked. They were exiting the highway—the Berkeley hills suddenly in front of her.

"Devon, we'll drop you off first." Maya said.

Devon sat up straighter, stretched, and forced herself to fully wake up. "Wait, no. I thought we were dropping you off first."

"I have to see Eric before the trial."

"That's today?"

Maya nodded.

"Then I'm going with you. Eric made me some promises, and trial or not, he's not backing out of them."

"Devon, I don't think you're really grasping what's going on today," Maya began impatiently, sounding very much like her mother. "There's—"

"Stop it. I sprang you from St. Mary's so you could get on the witness stand to defend a guy that killed his own brother out of greed. Trust me. I get the gravity of the situation."

"If you think we're so awful, why'd you come get me?" Maya asked, staring out the window.

"My scholarship is riding on it, remember?" Devon fumed. "Not like you'd ever know what this is like with a father like yours, but not everyone can afford a Keaton education. I need to get back in somehow. And besides, I actually think Hutch would have wanted me to."

Maya turned to her and blinked. Her lips quivered. The color had drained from her round cheeks. "Pacific Heights, then, please, Kevin," she said in an uncertain voice. "You can drop Miss Mackintosh off afterward." She paused. "Devon, thank you."

A LINE OF PARKED cars—none of them very fancy, all of them official-looking—took up the block in front of Eric's house. Of course; the trial began today.

Kevin pulled the SUV right into the driveway, which made Devon self-conscious. She wanted to be here but didn't want her arrival to be a major announcement . . . especially now that she knew that Maya was unaware of her scholarship problem.

Eric had blackmailed Devon without telling Maya the specifics. That was a problem. In a weird way, it humanized him even more. He knew things Devon didn't, but he didn't want Maya to be part of whatever sordid business lay at the heart of this mess, the business that endangered Devon herself. Devon smoothed back her hair and made sure she didn't have any crusted eye boogers or drool on her face. In the intervening silence, Maya had applied makeup and redone her elegant bun.

"I'm going in first," Maya stated, climbing out of the car.

"Whatever works." Honestly, Devon was grateful. She had no idea what they were walking into. Before she had even closed the door behind her, Bill and Mitzi Hutchins stepped out of the front door in crisp business attire. Spotting Maya, Mitzi put a hand to her heart and hurried back inside.

C.C. and Edward Junior Bolted through the front door moments later.

On instinct, Devon lunged back inside and closed the door behind her. C.C. wrapped her arms around Maya, eyes squeezed tightly shut; she shook her head as if fighting back tears. St. Mary's had definitely sounded the alarms. So had Keaton, probably . . .

Devon ducked down in her seat. Best not to be associated with Maya's dramatic return if she could help it—though it was probably too late for that. She was in this, totally and completely. She sat back up and peered out the window.

C.C. held Maya at arm's length, her voice getting louder. Maya shouted back, and C.C. slapped Maya across the face. Mitzi and Bill cringed along with Devon. She watched as they slipped back inside, and Edward Junior pulled C.C. away.

"We're fixing it. Why don't you trust me?" Maya screamed at her mother, loud enough to hear through the car windows. Eric appeared at the front door in a dark suit. Clutching her cheek, Maya ran into his arms. C.C. threw up her hands and turned her back on them. Her eyes narrowed and settled on the SUV. Devon's heart beat faster as she locked eyes with C.C.

"Let's go," Devon said to Kevin.

"You sure?" He shifted the car into reverse and backed out the driveway.

"I'm sure." Devon watched Eric as he ran to Maya, squeezing her close. In Devon's side mirror she could see Eric watching the SUV as it drove away. C.C. kept her gaze glued to the car. She yanked out her cell phone and stormed back to the house.

Devon sat straight in her seat as the car sped away from Hutchins Villa-turned-prison. Her phone buzzed in her pocket. It was a text from a number she didn't recognize.

Meet me at Huntington House tomorrow at 11. I know Eric had a role in convincing you to free my daughter. We need to talk.

CHAPTER 25

Mom was at work (or so she claimed), so Devon paced the house until Bodhi called at 8:53 in the morning. He was in a hurry, so she let him talk. Apparently he and Raven were on their way to Eric's trial. The prosecuting attorney wanted to demonstrate their relationship with Reed, to show why Reed would have changed his will and cut Eric out of his inheritance in favor of Hutch, creating Eric's motive for wanting Hutch out of the picture.

Bodhi would call with more as soon as he could.

Devon stared out the window after he'd hung up. She wondered if Eli or Khaki would appear. She had a feeling they wouldn't. Strange—even alone in the house, her future a question mark—she felt truly safe for the first time in a while.

∞

Bodhi's next call came at the stroke of five o'clock.

Eric Hutchins was found guilty of involuntary manslaughter and sentenced to three to five years in San Quentin, minimum security.

Devon wasn't sure how she felt, other than sick. Again, she listened as Bodhi relayed the proceedings: how Eric had cried over his addiction to his pain meds, his unstable thoughts, and his promise to attend rehab for as long as the judge wanted. Add that to Maya's teary defense of "the father of my unborn child, who arranged for me to be present to testify on his behalf," and the judge seemed to revel in the leniency.

Devon couldn't believe it. After everything, Eric would be across the Golden Gate on waterfront property. He'd probably spend those years working on his tennis serve.

"I figured your mission was a success," Bodhi concluded, out of breath.

"How?" Devon cried.

"Maya was there. You sprang her."

"Yeah, but I have no idea about my scholarship, and Maya's mom knows I'm the one that brought her back. She wants to have lunch with me tomorrow."

Bodhi drew in a sharp breath. "Just you and her? Jeez, that's intense. Why?"

"Wish I knew. It's at Huntington House. Should I just not go?" The more Devon thought about it, the idea of possibly bumping into Eli again seemed not only scary, but kind of reckless. Eric had successfully blackmailed her, and now he was certain of his fate. Maybe he had no intention of honoring his end of their bargain.

She felt the color drain from her cheeks. Of course he didn't. He was a psychopath.

"That's where you saw her before, right?" Bodhi asked. "And Eli was there? There's something about that place."

Devon fell onto the couch. "I know. I mean, I know rich people love having a club or something to go to, but it feels like something else."

"Tell you what, I'll take you over there tomorrow. I'll wait outside. No one will know I'm there. I don't want you there alone for something like that. Plus . . ."

"Plus?" Devon breathed.

"I kind of missed you," Bodhi said.

Devon glanced around her empty house, wondering again about her mother's conspicuous absence.

"I miss you, too," she said. "It's nice to be missed."

BODHI'S VW BUS WAS so glaringly out of place idling in front of Huntington House, that Devon was tempted to ask him to move it. With tired eyes, Devon looked up and down the block. She didn't see Eli or anyone suspicious. She realized her palms were sweating. She rubbed them against her "formal dress"—the same exact charcoal-gray one-piece she'd worn to her first interview with Mr. Robins to convince him to let her be a peer counselor.

It still fit. Actually, it was a little loose.

"I don't know why, but I'm nervous," she said.

Bodhi leaned out of the driver's-side window and kissed her cheek. "She's just a person. And she knows what you need to know. Besides, you look better than she ever could in a million years. That matters to people like her."

Devon smiled in spite of herself. "Thanks, that's totally not helpful."

"Go in there, see what she has to say, let her play her little game, and then you're out of there. I'll be circling the block. If you see Eli or anything that freaks you out, you text. It's a public place; she can't touch you."

"I wouldn't be so sure about that. I saw her slap Maya the other day when she came back from Montana. It was pretty gnarly."

"You're not Maya. You'll be fine. Now let's go get this over with." Bodhi kissed her again. "I'll be right here."

DEVON WAS RELIEVED THAT Zara wasn't working the front desk. She couldn't handle another fake smile. It was all she'd had with her mother since last night—fake smiles and meaningless chatter about how proud Mom was that Devon was owning up to her mistakes and facing an uncertain future.

Then again, Devon was just as guilty. She hadn't spoken to Ariel since the summer. Bullshit for bullshit, until the truth came out.

Devon stepped past the hostess podium. Weird—the entire restaurant was deserted, except for C.C. at a table near the window. The whole room seemed set up just for her. Because it probably was, Devon realized. That was the kind of money at stake—money that could drive a boy to kill his own brother.

"Ms. Tran?" Devon greeted her. She cringed at how timid she sounded and forced herself to stand taller as she approached.

C.C. took a sip of her iced tea and smoothed the napkin. "You can sit."

Devon pulled out a chair. Instantly a waiter appeared with a glass of water. Not Eli. He disappeared back into the kitchen without saying a word.

"My daughter has been telling you a lot of stories, it seems," C.C. said. She sounded hurried and kept fidgeting with her napkin. "Very convincing ones about needing to be rescued, or about being held against her will."

Devon thought carefully before she responded. It was like a session in a way. *Let the subject lead the conversation.* "She called me. I was just trying to help."

C.C. leaned back in her chair, eyes still on her napkin, a bitter smile on her lips. "Well, I'm just a terrible mother, and there's nothing to be done, is that right?"

"I never said that," Devon responded evenly. Yes, C.C. was a terrible mother. But when someone was angry, that anger often hid hurt. Maybe C.C. was feeling like an *underappreciated* mother. It would make sense, given her narcissism.

"How much do you know about your father, Devon?" C.C. asked.

Devon shrugged, wondering if Maya's mom was steering the conversation toward how she wanted to make up for being a bad mother by being a good grandma to the child of a convicted killer. "Not a lot. But that's by choice. My mom did the sperm bank thing. Says she really wanted a baby, and she was getting older, and she didn't want to wait for the right man to come along and miss her window."

"Yes, well, it is all about windows, isn't it?" C.C. said. "Your mom's a beautiful woman. She's smart. Do you really think she couldn't find a man?"

Devon bristled inwardly but was careful not to show it. "I don't know. She's got pretty exacting standards. I didn't know you knew her."

"I don't want to be the one to tell you this, but in a way, it's my right. Your mother didn't go to a sperm bank. She had an affair. With a married man. Someone who wanted to keep his mistakes quiet."

C.C.'s voice seemed to fade. Devon couldn't breathe. Was her phone ringing? No, it was that her stomach suddenly felt like it was on vibrate. Blood flooded to her feet, leaving her light-headed. She wondered if puking right here, right now, would be a problem in this deserted, awful place.

"I guess that makes you . . . illegitimate," C.C. continued. "It's a shame they don't say *bastard* anymore. That word sums it up so nicely." She took another controlled sip of her tea.

Is this witch lying to me? Devon wondered, her desperate thoughts swirling. It couldn't be true. Yet . . . if this was the truth, how did C.C. Tran of all people know?

But then it all clicked into place. The hate in C.C.'s eyes spoke the truth plainly, and lined everything up like a slot machine. *Ping, ping, ping.* C.C. knew this because she knew that Karen Mackintosh had had an affair with C.C.'s husband, Edward Dover, Jr. His was the voice on the other end of that line. It not only explained the terrible present, it explained everything about her mom's behavior for Devon's entire life—including her push for Devon to apply to Keaton.

"He paid for my scholarship," Devon whispered.

C.C. nodded. "I told him not to, but he wanted you to have the whole Keaton experience, I guess. Prepare you for life, opportunities, and all that."

"Oh, God," Devon mumbled. C.C. was right. Devon was *a bastard*. Images of sixteenth-century England and babies being dumped in gutters flashed through her head.

No, that hadn't been her childhood at all. Her mother loved her. Her mother wanted a future for her—and Dover had seen to that, she now realized. She was the illegitimate daughter he had been keeping tabs on.

C.C. Tran had every reason to make Devon squirm. Here she was, at school in the same dorm with her daughter, walking around as living proof—a reminder of her husband's infidelity. She was Maya Dover's half-sister. Jesus.

"Is it just me?" Devon asked. *Oh please, let it be just me.*

"As far as we know, yes. Just you."

"Then what happened on the boat? Was that you? Because of this? Some sick revenge thing?"

C.C. finished her tea and smoothed her skirt as if preparing to leave. "I'm sorry, dear, I don't know what boat you're talking about."

"Eli calling in for another waiter? Practically killing me? You wanted me out of the way. When that didn't work, you bribed Dr. Hsu to keep tabs on me—"

"What a fascinating life you must lead!" C.C. snapped, glaring at Devon. "Jocelyn is an old friend of mine from Princeton. I may have nudged the Keaton administration to have her come in for your sessions instead of that underqualified oaf, Henry Robins. What he's doing in that position, how they let you work with other students—it's frankly a lawsuit waiting to happen."

"So you set Dr. Hsu up to rat me out?" Devon almost felt as if she were back on the yacht, her legs giving out from under her, her head inches from the rail . . .

"She's not working there anymore, so there's nothing to tell, really. I think we've discussed enough for today, don't you think? Maybe you should head home and have a little talk with your mother." With that, C.C. stood.

"Wait," Devon said a little too loudly. "Someone attacked me and my friends. I deserve answers."

C.C. looked around as if embarrassed by Devon's outburst, even though there was no one else in the restaurant. "You know, young lady, Dr. Hsu had lunch at this very table, and she told me that she felt conflicted about you. Didn't want to be a party to your deception or something to that effect. Our arrangement ended then."

Devon leaned back and watched C.C. leave, her heels silenced by antique carpet, and then clattering on the polished wood.

Too bad she wasn't hungry. Huntington House probably served a great lunch. But even if she wanted to order, the waiter was nowhere in sight. She doubted he'd return for any reason other than to kick her out.

CHAPTER 26

Devon wasn't sure where to start. Bodhi waited patiently for her to speak, steering the VW into San Francisco traffic. But it didn't feel right to tell Bodhi about the discovery about her dad until she had confirmation from her mom. There was still a chance C.C. could be wrong. Devon knew it was probably a 1 percent chance, but regardless, she decided her mom should still be the first person she told.

"So? You going to keep me in the dark?" Bodhi finally asked.

"She doesn't know anything about Eli or the boat attack." Devon kept her eyes on the street ahead. "But I was right about Dr. Hsu."

"Wanna know why that's super interesting?" Bodhi asked, unable to contain his excitement over news he was clearly dying to share. Why couldn't everyone be as terrible as holding things back as he was? How could so many people be so good at keeping secrets—herself included? Wasn't it contrary to human nature?

"Not really," Devon deadpanned.

"I'm ignoring your sarcasm and telling you the goods, anyways. While you were in there with Medusa, Raven heard from our mysterious emailer."

Now he had her attention. "Wait, the one that emailed Isaac?"

"And being the stir-crazy, broken-footed genius that she is, Raven already traced the IP address. It came from where you just dined."

Devon's jaw dropped. "Are you serious? When did Raven get the email?"

"Like a half hour ago."

"Then he could still be inside. Park the car. We gotta go back and get in there." Devon was already halfway out the door before Bodhi pulled over. She ran toward the kitchen entrance she'd used with Cleo and Oz.

Bodhi caught up and closed the door behind them. They ducked behind the supply shelves. Cooks and sous chefs bustled around the kitchen chopping vegetables, marrying ketchup bottles, and cleaning stovetops. A lunchtime rush was underway; C.C. must have only booked the restaurant for a half hour or less. Just enough time to devastate Devon.

"There has to be an office down here," Bodhi said. "Come on." He took her hand and led the way. Around the corner, they spotted an open door. Bodhi darted forward, peeked inside, and turned to nod at Devon.

Holding her breath and her head high, she marched inside.

A guy was sitting at the computer in a tiny room with schedules and Post-it notes tacked all over the wall. He didn't turn around. "I know, I know. Those lemons aren't going to cut themselves."

Bodhi locked the door behind them. The guy swiveled around in his chair, showing his dimples as he smiled.

"You again," Eli said. He sounded bored. "I should have guessed."

"Me again," Devon said through clenched teeth.

"Who're you emailing, Eli?" Bodhi asked.

Eli sized him up, but his eyes were blank. "Are you a member of this club, dude? I doubt it. So why don't you two just get out of here before I have to defend myself against trespassers? I'd hate for anyone to get injured in the process."

Bodhi's hands tightened into fists. Devon could feel the anger radiating off of him; it matched her own.

"Hey, we're here to help you," Devon said, her breath coming fast.

"Yeah, how's that?" Eli asked.

"There's a lot of evidence pointing to you, Eli. An attempt on my life on New Year's Eve. Trespassing on private school grounds and injuring a Keaton student. We have your hat, and the DNA matches findings from the yacht." *Okay, that's a bluff, but worth a shot.* Eli didn't protest, however. "We've got emails between you and Isaac. Security-camera footage on the boat and at school."

Eli shook his head and gave Devon a crooked half-smile. "You think it's going to be that easy? You can't trick me into confessing anything."

"Fine, we'll take Isaac's word for it. Or his coworkers who can vouch for your presence that night."

The smile began to sag. He shot a glance at Bodhi.

"Or you can tell us who hired you, and we leave you alone. There's no way this all came from you. You don't have that kind of cash to offer someone like Isaac. I mean, five thousand dollars? That's gonna be hard to justify on your salary."

Eli shifted in his chair, tensing as if preparing to pounce.

"It's a pretty good offer, Eli," Bodhi said. "The last guy Devon confronted just got convicted for manslaughter. She's one-for-one. You want to add to that record? 'Cause we're happy to make it two-for-two. Your call."

After an excruciating ten seconds, Eli 's muscles relaxed. He nodded toward the computer. "That's her right there." He scrolled through the chain of emails. "She hasn't given her real name or anything. I've never seen her, but we have a drop spot. The members sometimes use our services for extracurriculars."

"Wait," Devon said. "This email was dated over a month ago, and then just yesterday she re-emerges to send this?"

Bodhi squinted at the screen. "'We're not done,'" he read. "That's all it says. No name—"

"Yeah," Devon interrupted, the slot machine in her brain clicking into place. "But who do we know that's been out of communication for the last month or so and suddenly came back to the city yesterday?"

Bodhi bowed his head. "Maya," he breathed, sounding as disgusted as she felt.

Devon glared at Eli, even though the glare was really meant for herself. "I can't believe I was so stupid. I let Eric talk me into getting her out of there." She pushed forward to the computer and started typing. "She's right. We're not done. We need to rendezvous today. One P.M. Urgent." She turned back to Eli. "Where is this drop spot you mentioned?"

Eli's dimples faded into a scowl. "Upstairs. Library. You shut us down, though, you're going to piss off people way bigger than this."

Devon looked at Bodhi. He shrugged. They'd figure out what Eli meant by that later. Devon finished her email and hit SEND. "Okay, so now we wait."

Eli stood, but Bodhi slid in front of the door.

"What?" Eli asked nervously. "You sent your email. You don't need me anymore. Let me at least get back to work."

"Sorry, man," Bodhi said. "Probably best if we hang out here until our meeting. You're too much of a liability."

Eli laughed and sat back down. "Whatever, amateurs."

"Maybe," Devon said. She stood with her back to the wall, facing him. "But if you're lucky, the amateurs might keep you out of prison."

WHILE THEY WAITED, BODHI sent the email to Raven, who started tracking down the origins of the account. Even though Maya was the most likely culprit, Devon didn't want to believe it until she saw Maya walk into that library.

Why Maya? She couldn't figure it out. Had Maya planned this to get back at Devon for getting Eric to confess? The thought that Maya was actually her half-sister and probably knew the truth about Devon hurt the most. But maybe the "why" was that simple. Maybe Maya had known about Devon her whole life, and had hated her illegitimate half-sister before they'd even met.

At 12:55 Eli led them upstairs. Above the dining room was an ornate hallway, private rooms lining either side. The library's thick mahogany double-doors stood closed at the opposite end.

"So what? Members hire you for their dirty work?" Bodhi asked. He studied the framed photos of older club members that dotted the walls between the doors.

Eli sniffed. "You'd be amazed how much people will pay for a little muscle."

"Saber," Devon said. "That's the email address. That's your little side group?"

Eli smiled and shook his head at Devon as he opened the door to the library. Inside, it was exactly as Devon expected, almost like a movie set. Massive shelves with leather-bound books, wingback chairs, and crystal decanters full of scotch. Bay windows offered a view of downtown.

Eli flopped into one of the wingback chairs with a *humph*. Bodhi opened a decanter. After sniffing the scotch, he gave a low, impressed whistle. Devon sat across from Eli. She knew she would fidget too much if she was standing, and she wanted to come across as calm and in control as Maya had while orchestrating this whole mess.

The brass door handle squeaked. Devon sat up straighter in her chair. The first thing she spotted was a leg wearing khaki. Her eyes shot up, and the red birthmark confirmed it. This was the same scary guy that followed her in Berkeley. Afraid, she reached a hand out for Bodhi, but he was already standing beside her with a protective hand on her shoulder.

Khaki's gaze switched from Devon to Eli. He backed up and reached for the door, but it was too late. Maya had already stepped inside.

She looked from Devon to Bodhi to Eli, struggling to put on a calm façade. Then she turned to Devon's mysterious stalker. "It's fine, Soto. Wait for me outside."

Khaki nodded and left.

Maya rubbed her bulging stomach and made her way to the tufted couch, awkwardly easing into the cushions with a groan. Her cheeks flushed. "So you two are friends now? When did this happen?" She was talking to Eli, ignoring Devon.

He stared at his scuffed black waiter's shoes.

"I think it was New Year's Eve when we first met," Devon growled. "Followed by a short meeting here in the kitchen, after which I met your good buddy, Isaac. Oh, and then Soto there stalked me across the bay. But then Eli came back and tried to run Raven over and steal her brother's car. Does that about cover it, Bodhi?"

She glanced up. His eyes were squarely on Eli, watching for any sudden move. "There's also a road trip to Montana," Bodhi said.

"Right, that whole game with my scholarship to get me to rescue you. I should have left you with the nuns and a shotgun. I'm sure you'd have been fine."

"So then you covered it all," Maya said. Her voice was toneless.

"How did you get them to yank my scholarship? Was that your mom?"

Maya shook her head. "I made a deal with my father once I found out who you were. He could send you to Keaton as long as you didn't make a claim to your inheritance. Once we saw that you found the original agreement, you'd be too unpredictable. He agreed you had to go. Off campus, that is. I would have preferred a cleaner, more permanent solution like the one I tried on New Year's Eve, but that's just my luck. Eli couldn't deliver."

Eli was studying his fingernails.

Devon tried to process the words. Maya's round belly and glowing cheeks made it difficult to grasp all the horror spewing from her mouth. *This girl is about to bring a life into this world. This sick, greedy sociopath . . .*

"What do you mean, the original agreement?" Bodhi asked.

Devon gasped. "You mean between Reed and Keaton and Dover?"

Maya tilted her head, her eyebrows arched, waiting for Devon to continue.

"Oh my God," she breathed. It hit her then: *Reed knew I'd never see the agreement unless I found the copy he'd hidden.* "All descendants have to agree. That's what this is. You don't want me to make a claim. You and Eric used the baby to bring your two families together. And with Hutch and Reed both gone, Keaton's descendants long gone, I'm the only one left that could possibly stand in your way."

Maya shrugged. "It was only a matter of time until you figured that one out. We knew who you were when you started Keaton. But Dad was ashamed of you, not that I can blame him. He was too cautious. He wanted to wait until he knew for certain that you knew who you were. I guess Reed told you everything, then?"

Bodhi leaned down and whispered in Devon's ear. "What the hell is going on? Am I missing something? Are you related to Edward Dover?"

Devon blinked up at Bodhi, forcing a smile as her eyes moistened. "Didn't have time to tell you. Weird, right?"

Maya rolled her eyes. "Don't worry, the feeling is mutual."

Eli stiffened, and Devon's ears perked up. Police sirens were approaching. They grew louder, followed by the screeching of tires and shouting on the street below.

"My sister called in the cavalry," Bodhi said, squeezing Devon's shoulder.

"Raven," Devon murmured. She kept her eyes on Maya, whose cheeks were now devoid of color. "Amazing what some siblings are capable of, huh? I wouldn't try to run in your delicate condition. You have your child to think about. Remember?"

CHAPTER 27

Raven and Devon's mother arrived at the police station only moments after Bodhi and Devon. Karen Mackintosh, mistress of Edward Dover, sat beside Devon during the sworn statement with the chief investigator. She and Mom needed time alone, but that would have to wait. And the statement was surprisingly easy, almost enjoyable. Devon didn't mind repeating every single detail of the attack on the boat, the stalking, what had happened to Raven . . . no, it was a pleasure. She had proof that her paranoia was founded in reality.

Raven submitted their gathered emails and security footage. When presented with the evidence, Maya's family attorney had started discussing a plea deal immediately.

Out in the waiting room, Devon ran to Raven first. Bodhi stood smiling as Devon tried not to hug Raven too tightly, given that she was limping with a plastic boot over her foot cast.

"You made it happen, Raven. You saved us."

"Hardly," Raven muttered, gently extricating herself from the embrace. "I was just trying not to miss out on all the fun. Plus, I really wanted to see Maya not get everything she wanted for once. That doesn't make me a horrible person, does it?"

"Hardly." Devon rolled her eyes at Bodhi. "How did you get here, anyways? You're not supposed to be driving."

Raven smiled, sheepish. "I hired a town car. I know it's a stupid rich person behavior, but man, it was so nice. I could totally get used to some of these perks."

"Um, so I'll call you later, okay?" Bodhi said. He grabbed Devon's shoulders and looked her in the eye. "We're not going to just let you disappear into some Berkeley cloud. I'll come visit next weekend, maybe."

Out of the corner of her eye, Devon sneaked a peek at her mom, who waited awkwardly in the hallway, trying to give them a little space. "Yeah, okay. I'll see you soon," she said.

Bodhi kissed her. "Family is never easy," he said gently. "So you don't have to worry. You'll get through it. It's over."

Only he could have made her believe something she doubted more than anything she ever had. The only thing she didn't have to worry about was him. But maybe for now, that was enough. She and her mom were just getting started.

THE CAR RIDE HOME was silent. Horribly silent. Finally, as her mother parked her car in the driveway, she broke the silence. "Devon, I owe you an apology. I should probably start there."

Heat moved down Devon's arms, her chest. Her heart began to beat quicker. And then she exploded. "How could you not tell me? How could you let me go to that school and be watched by them all the time? Didn't I deserve to know? You've been lying to me my whole life! How could you do that?"

A tear dripped down her mom's right cheek. She reached over

and wiped Devon's face. Devon hadn't even realized she'd been crying, too.

"I did what I thought I had to do. I knew I was playing with fire with Edward, but I never thought anything bad would really happen. And then I got pregnant with you, and I realized it was the best thing that could have happened. Edward and I agreed to stop seeing each other, but he didn't want you to disappear from his life. He couldn't be there, but he wanted to know about you. And . . ."

"And what?" Devon pushed.

"And I was in no position to turn down the money. I had to promise to keep his identity out of it. Forever." Her mom leaned back on her headrest and squeezed her eyes shut. Wet mascara marks streaked her cheeks. "I should have told you. I should have believed you at New Year's. I just never thought what position it might put you in." She held one of Devon's hands in both of hers and squeezed.

"So that phone number in your room?" Devon asked.

Her mom laughed a little through the tears. "You weren't supposed to find that, but I guess I forgot who I was dealing with. Edward had a private line just for me. He knew something was up when you called it."

Devon stared out the window. "So he really canceled my scholarship? Can I still not go back to Keaton? I was just looking where Reed wanted me to. It's nothing personal to him. I didn't even know what we were going to find."

"It's going to work out how it's supposed to. I don't know. I'm talking to him, though, okay? After Maya . . . I can't believe he raised such a little spoiled brat."

"Mom, she tried to have me killed." Devon whipped around to face her. "You're allowed to use harsher words than that."

"Oh, I have, don't you worry." The words were a hoarse whisper. Mom leaned close to Devon, almost conspiratorially. "But listen, can we tackle this stuff tomorrow? I haven't seen you in too

long. How about we get takeout? We can eat too much and watch
The Bachelor? I'm still looking for Mr. Right, you know."

Devon nodded, a lump in her throat. "Maybe you'll find him,"
she said. "If it can happen to me, it can happen to you."

HEADMASTER WYLER'S CALL CAME before the food arrived. "Next
week ends your suspension, and we'd love to welcome you back to
Keaton if you feel up to it," he said.

Devon stared at her mom, eyes wide. She silently mouthed his
name. Her mother dashed upstairs to grab the cordless from her
bedroom. Devon waited until she heard the click before continuing.
"Um, I'd love to, but don't we need to talk about financial aid or
something like that?"

He chuckled. "We could talk about financial aid if you want, but
I'm afraid that doesn't apply to you. You have a full scholarship,
Devon. You're covered. And I trust that the future will be much less
uncertain."

Devon's chin quivered. It felt stupid and childish, but the thought
of never going back hurt more than she expected. Her mom rushed
over from the bottom of the stairwell and wrapped an arm around
Devon's shoulder. She was crying again, not that Devon could
blame her.

"Is the scholarship from the same place it was before? Because
if it is . . ."

"No, Devon. It's actually a new scholarship that was just created. I'm not at liberty to tell you the donors specifically, but they
wanted it to be called The Reed Hutchins Memorial Scholarship.
And you're the lucky recipient until you graduate."

Devon could barely force the words past the lump in her throat.
"Okay, that's amazing. I'll be there on Sunday night. And Headmaster Wyler, I'm really looking forward to being back. I'm not
going to jeopardize that again."

Mom broke into her secret stash of Nutter Butters to celebrate.

CHAPTER 28

Monday, February 11, 2013

Devon nearly slammed into Dr. Hsu coming out of her office. "What are you doing here?" Dr. Hsu asked.

"Isn't this our regular time?" Devon asked, puzzled.

Dr. Hsu shook her head and ushered Devon back through the door. The office was in disarray, halfway packed and strewn with boxes. "I'm sorry they didn't tell you. Friday was my last day of work. I'm just clearing out my office today . . . I was on my way to phone my husband."

"Really?" Devon asked.

Instead of the closed-off, professional stare Dr. Hsu usually had, Devon saw the human being. It was the same glimmer of empathy Dr. Hsu had shown when she'd spotted Raven crying on Devon's shoulder.

"I should apologize. And I should also thank you." She laughed as if finally getting a joke. "You reminded me that coasting is never an option with this job. Easy doesn't really exist. You still think you want to be a therapist?"

"I don't know." Devon shrugged and sat on the edge of the familiar blue suede couch, now dusty. "Actually, that's a lie. I do. When I think about the future, I can't think of anywhere else I'd want to be than in that chair." She nodded toward Dr. Hsu's blanket, a rumpled heap on the seat cushion. "If someone had gotten to Maya Dover earlier, or Eric Hutchins earlier . . ."

"Maybe someone can get to their child," Dr. Hsu agreed.

Devon turned to her. "I'll make sure of it."

Dr. Hsu nodded. She opened her top desk drawer and pulled out a thin envelope. "If you're still interested, I wrote you a recommendation letter. Maybe you'll use it for Stanford, maybe not. Your call."

"But . . ." Devon's lips pressed into a tight line. She was still angry.

"I know you must hate me," Dr. Hsu said. "If you want to report me to the board, I'd understand. I didn't tell Maya's mother anything personal, you know. I never shared our confidences. Except the Vericyl. I couldn't watch that happen. You didn't need it. I'm not sure anyone does, but there's apparently a market for it. And I guess we both know how the Dovers think. Money, money, money."

"Thank you, I guess?" Devon said after a moment.

Dr. Hsu smiled. "That is more than generous. And more than appropriate. You'll be fine, Devon. You know what you're doing. Have faith in yourself."

Devon held out her right hand to shake. It seemed "appropriate" as well. But instead Dr. Hsu pulled her into a hug.

THE LONG RAIN SPELL was finally over. The clouds were burning off, and a soft morning breeze swept in from the ocean. Campus was silent, and Devon stopped in the middle of Raiter Lawn to feel the sun warm her face.

"Two weeks in Berkeley, and you come back a sun-worshipping hippie?" a voice called across the lawn.

Devon opened her eyes as Cleo plodded toward her. "Time in the real world is like dog years compared here," she said.

"I'm glad you're back." Cleo stopped a few feet from Devon. Her smile faded. "Oz went back to St. Matthews. Missed his girlfriend too much, it turns out."

Devon bit her lip. "I'm so sorry. I had to tell you . . . It sucks."

Cleo shook her head. "It sucks, but whatever. I'm glad you told me. I'm not totally sure I would have done that if I was you. It was the right call. Now can we please pretend to do homework while you catch me up on this Montana thing I heard about?"

Devon's eyes narrowed, fighting back the familiar rush of paranoia. "How do you hear about everything?"

"Like I'd tell you," Cleo whispered, squeezing her hand. Her eyes drifted.

A girl with a Keaton baseball hat and hoodie was approaching them from downhill. Devon didn't recognize her, but figured she'd just been away too long. The girl had long brown hair mashed under the cap, and a very sharp jaw. Her whole face was drawn. She looked . . . older. She smiled and waved.

"Devon?" the girl called.

Devon zeroed in on the waving hand—specifically its wedding ring. This girl wasn't a girl at all.

The woman planted herself in front of Devon and Cleo. It was clear now that she was in her mid-twenties at least. "Devon Mackintosh, you're served. Your mother, your legal guardian, has just been served with the same papers. Have a good day." She flashed a sour smile, shoved something in Devon's hands, then turned and hurried away.

Devon gaped at the retreating woman, unable to move as she vanished into a waiting sedan in the parking lot across Raiter Lawn. Devon didn't know what had just happened. Somehow she was holding a manila envelope. She turned to Cleo, who nodded quickly, her eyes wide.

"Open it," Cleo ordered.

These were legal documents of some sort; the formal language might as well have been written in Sanskrit. But Devon's eyes homed in on the one vital piece that made sense: *Lawsuit from Dover Industries against Devon Mackintosh. For her percentage of ownership of the Dover, Hutchins, Keaton trust.*

She was being sued by a corporation. Her father's corporation.

"Oh my God," Cleo whispered.

Devon turned to her friend. Funny, for the first time in a long while, she didn't feel frightened in the least. Not of secrets, not of lies, not of hidden motivations. She knew the truth now, and the truth was all she needed. Let them sue her. She didn't care about the money, anyway; nobody could touch the Keaton trust, and that would see her through high school. After that, the future was hers to make, on her own terms.

"Game on," she whispered to Cleo. "Game on."